B

Slocum scrambled as the ~~~~~~~~~~~ re-
peated shots from his six-gun. Slocum swung about, pulled
his rifle, and aimed at the crate of explosives next to the
man. His first round missed and whined off into the night.
The second hit the dynamite square on. For a moment,
nothing happened—then a giant windstorm lifted him and
threw him down the hill.

Somewhere along the way he lost his Winchester, but the
pain was so intense in his arms and face he hardly noticed.
He landed, rolled, and came to a halt as he was pelted with
rocks from above. Most were small, but one grazed his
forehead and knocked him back. Then the world turned entirely black, as a cloud of choking dust washed over him,
and he was buried in a rain of stone. . . .

JAKE LOGAN

SLOCUM

SLOCUM'S GOLD

MOUNTAIN

J
JOVE BOOKS, NEW YORK

THE BERKLEY PUBLISHING GROUP
Published by the Penguin Group
Penguin Group (USA) Inc.
375 Hudson Street, New York, New York 10014, USA
Penguin Group (Canada), 10 Alcorn Avenue, Toronto, Ontario M4V 3B2, Canada
(a division of Pearson Penguin Canada Inc.)
Penguin Books Ltd., 80 Strand, London WC2R 0RL, England
Penguin Group Ireland, 25 St. Stephen's Green, Dublin 2, Ireland (a division of Penguin Books Ltd.)
Penguin Group (Australia), 250 Camberwell Road, Camberwell, Victoria 3124, Australia
(a division of Pearson Australia Group Pty. Ltd.)
Penguin Books India Pvt. Ltd., 11 Community Centre, Panchsheel Park, New Delhi—110 017, India
Penguin Group (NZ), Cnr. Airborne and Rosedale Roads, Albany, Auckland 1310, New Zealand
(a division of Pearson New Zealand Ltd.)
Penguin Books (South Africa) (Pty.) Ltd., 24 Sturdee Avenue, Rosebank, Johannesburg 2196,
South Africa

Penguin Books Ltd., Registered Offices: 80 Strand, London WC2R 0RL, England

This is a work of fiction. Names, characters, places, and incidents either are the product of the author's imagination or are used fictitiously, and any resemblance to actual persons, living or dead, business establishments, events, or locales is entirely coincidental.

SLOCUM'S GOLD MOUNTAIN

A Jove Book / published by arrangement with the author

PRINTING HISTORY
Jove edition / May 2005

ISBN: 0-515-13943-2

JOVE®
Jove Books are published by The Berkley Publishing Group,
a division of Penguin Group (USA) Inc.
375 Hudson Street, New York, New York 10014.
JOVE is a registered trademark of Penguin Group (USA) Inc.
The "J" design is a trademark belonging to Penguin Group (USA) Inc.

PRINTED IN THE UNITED STATES OF AMERICA

10 9 8 7 6 5 4 3 2 1

1

The chilly autumn wind kicked up a fuss outside the Stolen Nugget Saloon, but inside, half-hidden in clouds of smoke and greed, the poker game grew hotter and nastier by the minute.

John Slocum leaned back in his rickety chair, eyeing the well-dressed man across the table from him. Playing poker had less to do with luck than it did reading the others in the game. To Slocum's right sat a drunken prospector who bet recklessly because it made him feel rich, even as every hand made him poorer. On the other side sat a tinhorn gambler Slocum had watched cheat by dealing seconds and even palming a card or two. The gambler had blanched a mite when Slocum had reached over, deliberately drawn his Colt Navy from his holster and laid it on the table, muzzle toward the gambler.

Slocum's hard green eyes had locked on the gambler's bloodshot, muddy brown ones, and that had been the last of the cheating. As far as Slocum was concerned cheating in this game was worse than dishonest, it was downright lazy. The other players bet foolishly and, like the prospector, had reasons to be at the table that had nothing to do with walking away richer.

Slocum needed the money and intended to win it fair and square, even if it felt as if the others were simply handing it to him. He had been on the trail for more than a month, stopping briefly in San Francisco before meandering northward and then cutting across California and heading for Geiger Pass. He had come to rest here in Truckee, California, because of the threat of a storm higher in the mountain passes. Snow fell early and hard in the Sierra Nevadas, and prudence dictated that he ought to let the weather clear before heading farther east toward Denver. Then? He had no idea where he would go when he reached the Queen City of the Rockies. And it hardly mattered, because he would be several hundred dollars richer in a few minutes thanks to the wild-eyed businessman sitting across the poker table.

Of all the men at the table, he was the one whose motives were most opaque to Slocum. He bluffed outrageously and lost, taking only small pots with decent hands. Slocum could not rule out the possibility that the man was priming the pump for this very hand. The man's expression told how close he was to flying off the handle. The money mattered to him—a lot. But he played poorly and might as well have written his hand on his forehead. Why did he play? Debts to pay? Prestige? Or simply for the thrill of it?

It did not matter to Slocum because he was going to win this hand and clean out the man's stake.

The bustle of the Stolen Nugget ebbed and flowed like the wind whining outside, but Slocum ignored it all. The man with the money looked prosperous enough and had nigh on five hundred dollars on the table. Slocum had won enough in earlier hands to raise him another ten dollars, but that would tap him out. The man was not going to let the pot slip through his fingers because he didn't have enough money to call Slocum.

Slocum rested his hands on the cards in front of him. He had no need to look at the full house, aces over queens, again. The businessman had something less but still a good hand. He wasn't bluffing and thought this was going to be his time to strike it rich. Slocum read it all on the man's face.

"Are you in or are you folding?" asked Slocum.

"I, uh, I don't have enough to call," the man said. Sweat beaded on his forehead. He had to win this pot and thought he would. Slocum knew he wouldn't.

"Then the pot's mine," Slocum said. He didn't reach for the chips, coins and greenbacks on the poker table because the man couldn't let it go that easily. There had to be a kicker. Slocum wasn't disappointed when it came.

"I own this here saloon," the man said, wiping his face with a fancy silk monogrammed handkerchief pulled from his shirt pocket. "It's worth more than the pot, but I'll put it all up."

"That so?" Slocum looked around. One or two of the men watching the game nodded without knowing it. The man did own the saloon.

"I own controlling interest. That there fellow behind the bar—Preston—owns the rest."

Slocum saw the sour look on Preston's face and guessed he didn't cotton much to getting a new partner. That would change soon enough. Slocum had no interest in running a gin mill and would sell out for a decent price. Unlike the saloon owner, the money in the pot was enough to sate his avarice. Slocum had the man pegged now. The man had to win to prove he was better than anyone else in the game.

"Let's see what you got," Slocum said. The man grinned and turned over his cards. Slocum nodded slowly as he stared at the full house. The man had kings and deuces. "Good but not enough this time." Slocum flipped over his hand, then reached for his six-shooter still on the table to emphasize his intention to collect what was his. The former owner of the saloon had lost more than money. He had lost face in front of a room filled with his regular customers.

"You got beat, Carnell!" From behind the bar came a

rollicking laugh. Preston's mirth grew until he had to hold his sides. "This is just desserts, Carnell. Get the hell out of the saloon. I never much liked you as my partner, anyway."

"Might be a good idea," Slocum said softly, hefting his ebony-handled six-gun.

Carnell shot to his feet, his face as stormy as the weather outside the saloon. He stalked from the smoky room, his boot heels clicking angrily until the wind drowned out the sound of him going down the boardwalk.

"How much of this place do I own?" Slocum asked Preston. The barkeep wiped tears from his eyes, fished under the bar for a bottle and a pair of shot glasses and came over to the table.

"You and me look to be partners," Preston said. "You bein' the senior partner. Carnell owned fifty-one percent and called the shots. No more!" Laughing at his small joke, the barkeep put the two shot glasses on the table and poured a healthy jolt of rye into each. He lifted his in salute to Slocum.

Slocum was slower to follow suit, wary of a Mickey Finn. He didn't know Preston or anything about how the Stolen Nugget Saloon was run and had always been skeptical about drinking with strangers. Preston seemed good-natured and honestly pleased at having a new partner. Seeing that Preston knocked back a second shot poured from the bottle with no ill effect, Slocum sipped at the rye whiskey, studied the man some more and wondered how Preston had become a bartender and part owner of a saloon. He had the same footloose look about him that Slocum did.

"How much do you reckon fifty-one percent of the Stolen Nugget Saloon is worth?" Slocum asked.

"You fixin' to sell out already? You can't! This place is a gold mine."

"Have places to go and things to do," Slocum said.

"I did, too, 'fore I came to Truckee and saw this place. I

decided to settle down, for a spell. The more I thought on it, the more I realized I had always wanted to run a saloon. This place catches the flow of gold and silver from the Comstock and greenbacks from the direction of San Francisco as financiers rush toward Nevada with money fallin' out of their coat pockets."

Slocum raked in the money he had won in the game and thought on it for a few seconds. Getting over the mountains at this time of year was tricky. Treacherous snowstorms blew in quick and left frozen bodies behind as grisly trail markers. The notion of going over Donner Pass always bothered him, even in the heat of summer. Eating your fellow man wasn't something that Slocum wanted to dwell on very long.

"That's a powerful lot of money, but you can double it in a month. That's a promise," Preston said.

"You make that much in a month?" Slocum had better than a thousand dollars on the table. Some of the scrip was probably worthless, issued on banks that had long since gone out of business, but the gold and silver coins accounted for a couple hundred dollars. He was richer than he had been in months.

"Twice that. Remember, we're both owners."

"I own controlling interest," Slocum pointed out.

"Not sayin' you don't," Preston went on as cheerfully as ever. "I could buy you out right now, but 'less I got you all wrong, you're a lot like me. I ain't stayin' here forever, but for the winter, maybe, haulin' in money hand over fist, that's all right. Warm in here, all the food and whiskey you want, there's a whorehouse down the street with mighty purty fillies in it. When you—when *we*—get tired, we can float off like a thistle on the wind, but with our pokes full of gold and silver."

Slocum thought Preston wasn't telling him everything. The barkeep had the feel of a man hiding out, or waiting for something to happen that he did not want to share with anyone else. It might be interesting finding out what it was, but Slocum wasn't that curious.

"I'll stick around until the storm blows over. Then I'll head out. You can buy my share then or I can ask around Truckee and find someone interested in making a pile of dough."

"The storm's likely to blow for three-four days," Preston said. "I almost got caught in one last spring comin' over from . . ." The words trailed off, as if he realized he was saying too much. Preston clamped his mouth shut and looked sharply at Slocum, as if he had gleaned the great secret from this slip of the tongue. Slocum made a point of ignoring what Preston had said as he counted through the greenbacks. He finished, then tossed them to Preston.

"Take this as operating money."

"You want gold back for it, don't you?" Preston asked slyly. "I knew you was my kind of gent. Discount rate's eighty percent. You got six hundred dollars in scrip, you get back one twenty."

Slocum nodded absently. The keyed-up feeling during the poker game had worn off now and left him drained. Finding a soft bed and a willing woman to help warm it over a frosty night was more important than dickering about how much he could get for worthless paper money.

"You take care of the business by yourself?" Slocum asked. "I need to find a place to spend the night. Got any suggestions?"

"Leila's got a bunk or two free, betcha," Preston said. "Not that she's *free,* if you know what I mean, but she's worth every dime she charges. I'll point you in the direction."

The two went to the door. Slocum grabbed to hold his hat in place as a gust of wind threatened to steal it off his head. Preston stepped out and pointed down the street. Slocum turned to look and saw the expression on Preston's face. Then the barkeep wrapped his arms around Slocum's shoulders in a powerful bear hug. His weight bore Slocum backward, and the two crashed hard to the dusty street. The instant they hit Preston was rolling and getting to his knees, his six-shooter coming out from a shoulder rig slung so his pistol rode hidden under his left arm.

Slocum rolled in the other direction and stayed flat on his back. He fumbled for his Colt Navy but was clumsy, slow—and looking at imminent death. Carnell stood on the boardwalk with a scattergun leveled at him.

Slocum cringed as the report echoed forth, caught on the wind and was immediately swallowed. For an instant Slocum simply stared. Then he rolled to his right, got his six-shooter out and came back ready to fight, but by this time Carnell had slumped to a boneless pile in front of the saloon.

Out of the corner of his eye Slocum saw Preston holding his six-gun in a rock-steady hand.

"Thanks," Slocum said.

"I saw him comin' to shoot you in the back. Sorry if I roughed you up gettin' you out of his sights," Preston said. He climbed to his feet and cautiously advanced, his pistol never leaving the corpse. Slocum appreciated a vigilant man. One who had saved his life with a deadly accurate shot was even more prized.

"Thanks for drilling him when you had a chance," Slocum said. "With that sawed-off shotgun, he couldn't have missed me."

"Always knew Carnell was a no-account snake in the grass but never thought he'd shoot anyone in the back."

"That's a good way of keeping down the return fire," Slocum said dryly. He poked at Carnell with his toe. The man was deader than a doornail.

"Don't know about you, Slocum, but I can use a drink. On the house."

"It's fifty-one percent my house," Slocum said, laughing. He clapped Preston on the shoulder and the two went inside, out of the wind that tugged fitfully at the dead man's clothing.

Slocum wasn't sure how long they sat drinking, swapping lies and getting to know one another. The more Preston talked, the more Slocum liked the man. They had similar backgrounds, even if Preston had fought for the North in the Sixth Pennsylvania. Slocum wasn't sure but the two of them might have swapped lead at a skirmish or two during the war. After Appomattox, their histories were almost identical. Legal chicanery had driven both of them off family farms and put them on the road westward. Preston never came right out and said he had engaged in a bit of highway robbery, but Slocum caught the hints. He had been known to rob a stage or two in his day, too, when the need arose.

Cut in between their increasingly drunken reminiscences were thirsty customers demanding service. Somehow, no matter how much he drank, Preston capably dealt with the paying clients. Sometime around an hour till dawn, the wind died down to a mournful howl and the last of the paying customers stumbled from the Stolen Nugget Saloon. Slocum sat in the same chair where he had won the saloon from Carnell, not quite drunk but far from sober. He wondered how long it would take before someone noticed the former owner's body outside and brought it to the marshal's attention.

He was about to ask Preston about the law and how it was enforced in Truckee when he saw movement out of the corner of his eye. Slocum turned in the chair at the same instant a gunshot rang out. Going for his pistol, he knocked over his chair. The cowboy who had shot Preston swung around, startled. He obviously had not expected to find anyone else in the saloon.

The gunman started firing, and Slocum foolishly tried to dodge. Unsteady on his feet, he staggered and then hit the floor. Wiggling along like a fish out of water, Slocum sought cover behind the dilapidated piano at the back of the room. By the time he sighted down the barrel of his six-shooter, Preston's killer was nowhere to be seen.

Slocum listened hard and heard mumbled curses. Then, plainer than day, "Where is it, damn your eyes! Tell me!"

The gunman was hidden behind the bar, crouching over Preston. Slocum inched along the wall, sucked in a breath, steadied himself, then popped up and aimed down at the floor behind the long mahogany bar. The owlhoot had rifled through Preston's pockets and held a crumpled sheet of paper.

"Drop it!" Slocum ordered as he squeezed off a shot. He saw that the man wasn't going to obey and would ventilate him if he didn't shoot first. Lead sailed past Slocum's head, causing him to instinctively duck.

This was enough to disturb Slocum's aim and let the man scamper around the far end of the bar to escape into the early morning. Slocum recovered his balance and went after the man, but when he got to the door, the street was empty save for Carnell's corpse.

Disgusted, Slocum went back into the saloon and rounded the bar. To his surprise, Preston stirred, moaning weakly. Slocum dropped to his knees and rolled the man over so his head rested on a dirty bar rag.

"Does this town have a doctor? Hold on and I'll fetch him," Slocum said.

"No, wait." Preston reached out with a surprisingly strong grip and held onto Slocum's coat. "He took it. He stole it. Son of a bitch."

"Who was it? Do you know who shot you?"

A powerful shudder rippled the length of Preston's body, and his tanned face drained of blood. Slocum had seen this before. Preston was dying and there was nothing anyone this side of heaven could do to help him.

"Slocum, he took the map. Get it back, give it to my

brother. Virginia City. Brother's in Virginia City. Map. Please!"

"Settle down now," Slocum said. "Don't excite yourself."

"Promise me. You owe me. I saved your life."

"I'll do it. Now—"

Slocum looked down into the sightless eyes and knew Preston had succumbed. He rocked back on his heels and swore steadily at making such a damn fool promise to a dying man he hardly knew. Then he stood and walked into the cold dawn of a new day.

2

Slocum stared at the slowly awakening town of Truckee and wondered where he should start hunting down the man who had killed Preston. Promising to retrieve the map—to what?—and give it to Preston's brother in Virginia City was about the stupidest thing Slocum had done in quite a while, but honor forced him to try to find the killer. If nothing else, he could bring the back-shooting son of a bitch to justice since Preston hadn't had a chance to defend himself. Slocum considered what he might have done now if Preston had not saved him from Carnell earlier in the night. He heaved a sigh of resignation as he realized he would still be on the murderous owlhoot's trail because it was the right thing to do.

At the thought of former saloon owner, Slocum walked over to where Carnell lay slumped and stared at the rigid body for a moment. No one had raised a ruckus about the corpse yet. Slocum gave it a hearty kick to vent his displeasure at what had begun this chain of events forcing him to track down a killer, then settled his Colt Navy in its crossdraw holster and headed down the street for the livery stables. He doubted the pusillanimous dog who had killed

Preston would remain in town, especially since the sheet of paper had been his goal.

"A treasure map," Slocum grumbled as his long stride devoured the distance to the stables. In his days roaming the West he had come across dozens of bogus treasure maps. Most had been harmless enough frauds, but some had led the men buying them to their deaths. He calmed a mite and tried to remember Preston's exact words. Treasure had never been mentioned, but then not much else had, either. What was his brother's name? Virginia City was a boomtown with men coming and going constantly. Not knowing a name to ask after, Slocum might as well be hunting for a needle in a haystack.

His only consolation was that Preston hadn't said it was a map to some lost gold mine. It might be a map showing something else entirely, though Slocum couldn't imagine what that would be. He got hotter under the collar as he walked, until he came to realize anger wasn't going to let him discharge his duty any faster. He had to stay cool and collected and use his head if he wanted to fulfill his promise to Preston. Then he could ride his own trail again.

Slocum trudged to the livery and heard coming from the rear the steady clang of a hammer on iron. He walked around the stables, and a blast of heat told him the smithy was already hard at work, although he didn't immediately see him.

"Anybody here?" Slocum called, even though he had heard the heavy hammer pounding hot iron into shape. Movement at the rear of the shed alerted him to the smithy's presence. He walked around the open hearth to see a man crouched by a bucket of water with long metal pincers in his hand. Steam rose from the bucket where he quenched his work. The man pulled out his prize, a large horseshoe, and examined it critically before looking back at Slocum.

"You're the new saloon owner, you and Preston," he said. Seeing Slocum's suddenly wary expression, he hastily added, "News travels fast in this here town. My brother was in the saloon last night when you won with that ace-high full house. What kin I do fer ya? Need some fancy wrought-iron work done to fancy up the ole Stolen Nugget?"

"Didn't know you were the town blacksmith when I left my horse in the stable," Slocum said. His mind turned over things and came to a quick solution to some of his problems. "There's been a peck of trouble. Preston's been killed and so has Carnell. I'm going after Preston's killer."

"Do tell." The smithy stood. He was half a head taller than Slocum's six feet and outweighed him by a goodly fifty pounds. Not an ounce of that was fat.

"I couldn't find the marshal," Slocum said, trying to weasel out of a complete explanation. The more he had to explain, the more likely he was to end up in the hoosegow until after an investigation. Truth to tell, Slocum wasn't eager to prove his innocence since he had fired enough times at Preston's murderer to make it look as if he might be the one who had killed his new partner. Trying to convince anyone that Preston had killed Carnell in an act of self-defense was even less likely since Preston was dead. While Slocum figured he might have outrun a warrant on his head for killing a federal carpetbagger judge back in Georgia, he didn't want to find out.

"Not likely you will. Ain't got one in town right now. Last one was caught tryin' to rob the bank, so we hung him. Mighty hard findin' anyone to take the job after that."

Slocum tried not to look too relieved. There wouldn't be a lawman sniffing around, trying to figure how Carnell died or why Slocum had not bothered to report his or Preston's death. Tedious explanations no law officer would believe in a month of Sundays were to be avoided if he wanted to catch the killer.

"You know anyone trustworthy enough to run the Stolen

Nugget Saloon for however long it takes me to track down the varmint that murdered Preston?"

"Reckon he *was* yer partner," the smithy said, rubbing his stubbled chin with meaty fingers. "That makes it yer duty to find the killer, don't it? Good to see honorable men comin' through town these days. Too many don't have a lick of sense, much less respect for the dead."

Slocum held his tongue, seeing the smithy was working over something more than a comment on moral men. He wanted to hear what it was.

"You know, it might be that gent what rode out of town ten minutes back. Headed toward the mountains." The muscular man shook his head so hard that sweat flew off in bright beads. "Damn poor time to try to git through the pass with that storm on us." Punctuating his words, a sudden cold blast of wind made the heat seem more inviting than it had been.

"Toward the Sierra Madres," Slocum said in disdain. Only a tenderfoot or a desperate man would try to cross the mountains now. In a few days, after the storm blew itself out, would be a better time to attempt crossing through a pass.

"Yep."

"Better get into the saddle," Slocum said. "I've got quite a head start to overcome."

"What kinda deal you makin' for the saloon?" the smithy asked.

"You know anything about saloons?"

"Hell, I was born in one." The smithy laughed. "You put me in charge and I'll turn you a good profit. That brother of mine can look after it when I'm not there. Or I can buy it outright."

That was as good an offer as Slocum was likely to get for the Stolen Nugget Saloon. They haggled a spell, but Slocum was anxious to get on the trail and sold out for a fraction of what the place was worth, if Preston had been telling the truth. He thrust out his hand and shook, his hand vanishing in the smithy's ham-hock-huge one.

Slocum saddled, took some supplies from the livery stables and turned his horse's face toward the mountains. They looked near enough to reach out and touch in the cold morning air, but Slocum knew it was a hard day's ride just to reach the foothills.

"Take care of Preston, will you?" Slocum called. "Money's in the till for that. It's not right for him to end up in the potter's field."

The smithy wiped his hands on a dirty rag and waved as Slocum trotted off, eager to begin the chase and even more eager to end it.

The wind couldn't get any colder. That was what Slocum thought until a new gust whipped down from the summit of the Sierras and cut like a razor at his cheeks and eyes. He pulled his bandanna up a little more over his nose to keep it from getting frostbitten. As abruptly as he had left Truckee, he had not gone on the trail poorly equipped. His heavy coat rode under his canvas duster, giving double protection against the heat-sucking wind. Roper's gloves provided some protection to his hands, but his fingers still tingled from the cold, and he wasn't sure about his toes. He tried wiggling them, but his boots felt as if they squeezed down hard all around his feet. As long as he had some sensation, he wasn't running much risk of losing a toe or two, but if the temperature dropped even more that was exactly what would happen.

He might be lucky if a couple toes were all he lost.

Squinting into the wind, eyes tearing up in reaction to the cold, he peered at the ground the best he could. The tracks left by the fleeing killer had been distinct enough close to Truckee. By getting out quick enough, Slocum had found the freshest hoofprints and followed them. By the time the sun actually poked up over the tall, sheer moun-

tain range, commerce along the road would have wiped out
any vestige of tracks. Wagons rolled constantly in and out
of Truckee, heading downslope toward San Francisco and
coming in from that port city with a steady flow of
prospectors looking to make their fortune in the Comstock.

It was late enough in the year that only the most intrepid
or stupidest would try crossing the Sierras now, but there
were enough. Slocum had a start on them as he caught
sight of a steaming pile of horse dung. He was less than
twenty minutes behind Preston's fleeing murderer.

A sudden powerful gust almost unseated him. He had to
gentle his horse to keep it from shying. Slocum felt he
wasted precious time soothing the animal's frayed nerves,
but the skittish horse was all that would keep him alive in
the worsening weather.

"Come on, let's walk a spell," he said, dismounting.
Slocum felt stabs of sharp pain in his feet as he led the
horse up the steep slope. He knew he ought to have done
this earlier. He needed the effort to keep his blood flowing
to his feet and hands so he wouldn't freeze to death by
inches. Being partially protected by the horse's bulk kept
him warm, also, but the horse struggled. The altitude was
more than the horse was used to, coming from sea level as
they had, and the temperature was turning downright polar.
The effort it took simply to keep moving increased, but
Slocum was determined. If he let the killer get away now,
he might never find him.

"Get the map. Give it to my brother in Virginia City,"
Slocum mocked. Either—or both—promises might have to
be broken, through no fault of his own. Even if he recovered the map, finding Preston's brother might not be possible. Not for the first time Slocum wished he had only tried
to ease the dying Preston's mind rather than making such a
rash promise. A promise to a dying man was inviolate. Always had been and always would be, as long as Slocum
drew a breath.

Coldness welled inside Slocum when he realized he didn't even know if Preston was the man's first name or last. How did he ask around Virginia City for a man who had a brother named Preston? Miners were sociable creatures if they were liquored up enough, but they were always cantankerous, unpredictable as old dynamite and never took kindly to anyone asking too many questions.

"Keep moving, damn it," Slocum said, lowering his head to take the new gust of wind against the crown of his hat. The brim folded down and flopped against ears and face, but he hardly noticed. He pulled up the bandanna a bit more and knew he looked like a train robber. But out here, with no other living being in sight, no one was likely to pay him any mind.

It was the kind of place he could die and never be found until spring.

"Don't stop walking," Slocum said, irritation rising. He swatted his horse on the rump to keep it putting one hoof in front of the other. Then he began to wonder if he ought to give up and go back to Truckee while he still had all his bodily parts.

Snowflakes, large and wet and cold, began pelting him.

After enduring another hundred yards of the increasingly intense wind and snow, Slocum was prepared to give up. Then he topped a rise and saw his quarry across a broad, grassy meadow half-white with new snow. Slocum judged distances and knew he could overtake the man if he tried.

"Come on," Slocum said, remounting the balky horse. "Give me some speed. After we settle accounts with him, we can go back to Truckee and I'll give you all the oats you can eat." The horse turned its face and looked back with great skepticism. Slocum used his spurs to get the horse moving into the teeth of the gathering storm.

The rider was hardly a mile off, but Slocum had misjudged both the time it would take and the trouble caused by the snowstorm. He reached the meadow and found the other horse's tracks were cut into a thin layer of snow and ice. That told him the temperature was much colder than he had anticipated. If the ground had been warmer, the snow would have melted and the tracks would have been half-frozen in mud.

A white curtain drew across the land, obscuring Slocum's view of the far side of the meadow where he had spotted the rider. The snow wasn't wet enough yet to stick, and it blew about like dust. The continual pelting of the fine, dry flakes caused his horse to start crow-hopping on him, but he kept control as he peered down at the ground to be certain he wasn't veering away from Preston's killer.

As he struggled across the meadow, a nagging worry slowed him. There might be any number of men on this trail other than the gunman responsible for Preston's death. Then Slocum realized such doubt would prevent him from ever getting back the map and bringing the true killer to justice.

He instinctively reached across and patted the lump made by his Colt under his duster and heavy coat. It rode where it was out of the snow and kept warm by his body heat, but getting it out when he needed it would be a chore. Slocum left the pistol where it was as he pressed on into the blowing snow.

"Hey!" he shouted when he saw the rider ahead, stopped on the rise at the far side of the meadow. He waved to attract the man's attention. Anything that slowed him would give Slocum a better chance of overtaking him.

Slocum had not anticipated the man's next action. Slipping between the dancing snowflakes came a rifle bullet that knocked Slocum from the saddle.

3

Needles thrust into Slocum's face, causing him to recoil. He turned and got a mouthful of dirt and snow. Spitting, he pushed back and came to his hands and knees, still not knowing where he was or what had happened. Slowly it all came back. He shook himself like a wet dog, got to his feet and took a few shaky steps. Snow whirled wildly about him and disoriented him. Slocum staggered a few paces, then stopped because he had no idea where he headed.

A shaking gloved hand touched the side of his head and came away bloody. The stark contrast of red blood against white snow shocked him into alertness. He straightened and checked to be sure he wasn't otherwise wounded, beyond the crease on his temple. The worst of his injuries were bruised ribs from falling off his horse.

Remembering his horse, he shucked off his gloves and put his fingers in his mouth, warming them for a moment, then venting a long, loud whistle to bring the horse running. Slocum heard nothing over the whine of the wind. For the first time, the seriousness of his predicament hit him. Without a horse, he was stranded and without supplies. If the storm got worse, he might freeze to death. Even if it didn't turn into a blizzard, he still ran the risk of dying from exposure. A man out in the wind for a long time was seductively drained of heat until it seemed normal not to feel fingers or toes.

Slocum whistled again and listened hard for any response from his horse. Nothing. He knew then he had to find shelter on his own or he was a goner. The first thing he had to do was figure out where he was. Dropping to his knees, he scraped away some of the accumulated snow and then walked in a wide circle to determine which way the land rose. He had been heading across the meadow when he was shot out of the saddle, and he intended to continue that way since he knew there was no shelter to be found on his backtrail.

Keeping the wind chewing at his left side, Slocum pulled down his hat and began trudging until he was certain he walked uphill. When he found faint traces of fresh hoofprints, his heart raced. It was either his horse or the one ridden by the man he pursued, since not much snow had piled up along the rims of the print. Slocum walked a little faster, keeping his arms swinging so the blood flowed freely through his limbs and kept them from tingling with cold. He made good time—then the ground fell out from under him.

Slocum keeled over and rolled and rolled and rolled until he fetched up hard against a large rock. Dazed by the sudden impact, he tried to stand but couldn't find the strength. His head hurt, his body ached and his legs were so rubbery he might never get to his feet again. But there was one bright spot amid all the damage done to his body. Being on the lee side of the boulder cut off the worst of the freezing wind and gave him a chance to recover.

He turned and saw movement in the thick blankets of snow whipping past him. Slocum yelled but his voice sounded muffled, as if someone had stuffed a rag into his mouth. He shouted again, struggled with renewed determination and got to his feet. As fast as he could move, he plunged into the storm.

"Here!" he shouted, though his voice came out a hoarse croak better suited to a bullfrog's throat. "Come back. Come on!" He slipped and slid in his haste, but the dark figure loomed ahead, beckoning him on like some half-seen Lorelei amid treacherous rocks. For once luck favored him. His horse's reins caught in a low-growing bush, preventing the animal from running off.

Slocum grabbed for the reins, caught them in clumsy fingers and then worked his way back, patting the horse with his snow-encrusted glove, soothing the skittish behavior and finally reaching the saddle. He grabbed the horn and pulled hard, getting himself belly down over the saddle. From here he swung about and properly sat astride the horse.

"View's no better from up here," he said, looking out into the whiteness cloaking the world. At least he no longer had to force his legs to move. He guessed at directions, using the wind as a compass needle, and urged the horse forward. From the way it strained, Slocum knew they made their way upslope. Now and then the rocks would break apart the onslaught of the storm and give him a decent view of the terrain. Rocks. Everywhere rocks.

Then he found salvation. Slocum tugged hard on the reins and guided the horse toward the base of a towering bluff that vanished into the storm above. The wind shear along the face of the cliff was vicious, but Slocum knew there had to be caves carved into the mountainside. Luck still rode at his shoulder. He found a shallow depression within minutes, dismounted and led his horse inside so it was trapped at the rear of the small cave.

"Time for a fire, if I can rustle one up," he said. Rubbing his hands together to keep the circulation, he scouted a few yards away and found enough dried wood for a fire. Lighting it was more of a problem with the invisible fingers of the wind caressing the rock around the cave mouth and occasionally sneaking inward, but he eventually succeeded. The tiny fire blazed merrily so he could warm his hands.

The next thing Slocum did was melt snow and put the water into his hat for the horse to drink. By this time, Slocum was exhausted. He had been caught like this before and knew he dared not slip off to sleep, not before he put more wood on the fire and ate. Keeping up his strength and doing all he could to retain bodily warmth would see him through the storm.

Hunched over, arms circling his drawn-up knees, Slocum finally allowed himself to slip off into a troubled sleep populated with gunfire and treasure maps caught on a high wind and blood drenching everything.

The storm blew itself out sometime during the night. When Slocum awoke, the entire world had turned white with a blanket of untrammeled snow. His arms and legs ached mercilessly, but he forced himself to stretch and work out the pain. He rebuilt the fire and melted more snow and let the horse drink greedily.

He left the dubious shelter of the shallow cave and found clumps of grass poking up enticingly through the snow. He put hobbles on the horse by this meager fodder and let it graze the best it could while he went back to his hardscrabble camp to boil some coffee and fix his own breakfast, which turned out to be more of the same hardtack and beans as the previous meal. Food had never tasted better.

Belly full and the aches a distant memory, Slocum felt like he could whip his weight in wildcats. Remembering why he had come out into this early storm, he worked through layers of clothing and drew his Colt to be certain it was still serviceable. Satisfied that the night cold had not impaired it, Slocum worked it back through his duster and

coat to rest easily on his left hip. Then he finished the re-
mainder of his tepid coffee and knew it was time to get on
the trail.

Either his quarry had gone to ground as he had to
weather the worst of the gale or he lay dead along the trail.
Nobody kept moving through such a powerful late autumn
storm for long.

Slocum mounted and rode about in the sharp sunlight,
hunting for the trail he had followed the day before. Snow
veiled everything, but the vee-shaped depression leading
downhill to the west showed the course of his tracks. The
snow slumped into the trail itself going up into the hills,
giving him his bearings again. Slocum sighted in on several peaks jutting proud and sharp in the distance before
getting his horse moving in a slow walk eastward.

He lost track of time, but the sun was over his shoulder
by the time he found tracks on top of the snow. Slocum
bent low and examined them from horseback, seeing no
reason to study them closely. He had found either Preston's
killer or someone else caught by the storm. If the latter,
Slocum knew the traveler would have noticed any other
rider out and about. One way or another he would find the
man who had gunned down Preston and then recover the
stolen map.

Slocum judged the length of the horse's stride and saw
an unevenness to the gait that signaled trouble. Some of the
horses making the trip to the Comstock were not shod—it
was expensive getting a set of shoes for a horse and many
prospectors were stone broke. Buying equipment and the
supplies necessary to keep themselves alive tapped them
out. But from the impressions Slocum saw, this horse carried a full set of shoes. Or it had when it began the trip into
the Sierras. Somewhere along the way it had thrown a
horseshoe and now hobbled.

That made it easier to overtake the rider. Slocum spotted him less than an hour shy of sundown. Any question of

the man's identity was erased when he turned, spotted Slocum and tried to get his horse into a gallop to escape. The horse balked and almost threw the rider.

"Give up!" Slocum shouted. His words carried through the cold, crisp air and bounced off distant hills in ghostly echoes. This only spurred on the man in his attempt to get away.

When Slocum saw the man dragging out his rifle, he drew rein and waited. Shooting from horseback was hard, and the shot that had taken Slocum out of the saddle back in the meadow had been more lucky than expert. The man swung about and fired five times. Not a single slug came anywhere near Slocum this time.

"You're going to hang for killing Preston," Slocum shouted. The echoes died about the time the man forced his horse into a canter. Slocum followed at a more sedate pace, knowing what would happen. By the time he reached the spot where the man had fired on him, the shoeless horse had pulled up lame and stranded its rider.

A hundred yards separated them. Slocum drew his Winchester and took careful aim. Years of experience and the cold calm of a trained sniper gave him a clean shot. The man yelped and clutched at his leg as he tried to scramble into rocks to make his stand.

Slocum's second slug spattered across the rocks above the man, causing a minor avalanche that bore him back to the trail amid dust and gravel. A new round jacked into the chamber of the Winchester, Slocum approached cautiously. The man was befuddled and tried to shake off his confusion at all that was happening. That made him as dangerous as a cornered rat.

"I'll kill you. By God, I thought I had killed you back in the meadow. You ain't gonna get it. It's mine, damn you, mine!" The man fired wildly. One round caused his horse to rear. In his panic, the man turned and fired point-blank

into the horse's belly, bringing it to the ground with a con-
vulsive shudder. It hit hard, kicked once and died.

Slocum's luck continued to hold. After he had settled
accounts with this yahoo, he would have had to shoot that
horse. It had pulled up lame and would never have been
good again. Without wanting to, the man had done the right
thing and put his own horse out of its misery.

Now it was time for Slocum to afford Preston's murderer the same fate.

He snugged the butt plate on the Winchester against his
shoulder and squeezed off another round. His target moved
at the last instant and did not sustain any injury. But the
shot sent Preston's killer scrambling over his fallen horse
to take refuge behind it. Slocum saw the rifle barrel rest on
the saddle as the man hid. His chance for an easy resolu-
tion was past. The man had twelve hundred pounds of carcass protecting him now.

Slocum jumped to the ground and led his horse down
into a draw where it would be safe and then fumbled
around in his saddlebags for more ammo. He dumped a
box of cartridges into his coat pocket before scrambling
back up the gravelly slope to the trail. Slocum half expected the owlhoot to have tried to escape, but the rifle barrel still poked over the side of the dead horse.

"Come on out and I won't shoot you. I will take you
back to Truckee to stand trial for killing Preston, but I
won't kill you here." Slocum knew the man would never
fall for such an offer. Better to die cleanly with a bullet in
your heart under the clear California sky than to take a
drop from a gallows platform, noose knotted around your
neck and a crowd jeering as you died. What he wanted was
for the man to rise up enough for him to get a decent shot,
but the murderer refused to take the bait.

Slocum edged closer, then froze. Something was
wrong, deadly wrong. He threw himself to the far side of

the trail, crashed into the stony path and kept going as a hail of bullets rained down on him. Slipping and sliding down the far slope, he finally caught himself and swung around, rifle aimed back toward the trail.

A cold lump formed in his belly. The killer was smarter than he had thought. Not only had he decoyed him into believing he cowered behind the dead horse while he circled and tried to gun Slocum down from behind, he had gotten between Slocum and his horse down in the ravine. Cursing, Slocum dug his toes into the shale and powered his way back up to the trail in time to hear his horse whinny in protest.

Rather than go chasing down the far side of the trail into the arroyo where he had left his horse, Slocum spotted a large boulder and scaled it in time to see the outlaw mounting and trying to keep the horse under control. The horse had a natural crow hop to it and used this technique to throw the unwanted rider about. From the way he flopped around Slocum knew that Preston's killer had never busted broncs.

Slocum raised his rifle to his shoulder and bided his time. Eventually the man got control of the horse and started up the ravine, away from the trail. Slocum squeezed off a perfect shot that caught the man smack dab in the middle of the back. Arms flying upward, the man tumbled off the horse and fell into the rocky ravine.

Slocum had no choice but to make a killing shot. From this distance, with his target on a bouncing horse, it would have been folly to try to wing the rider. Even if he had succeeded, the man might have ridden off with lead in a shoulder or leg. Sliding down the curve of the boulder Slocum landed hard on his feet, staggered a few paces and then broke into a lope to reach the man's side. Either he would recover soon enough so Slocum could finish him off, or he might cling long enough to life to blurt out a few words that would help Slocum find Preston's brother.

If he was dead, fine.

Slocum slowed his run and approached cautiously. His Winchester aimed squarely on the recumbent form, he circled and came up so he could kick away the six-shooter near the man's hand. Only then did he kneel and grab the man by the shoulder to roll him over.

Slocum's marksmanship was proven again. The bullet had caught the fleeing killer in the spine, smashed through and exited his chest. Any of a half dozen resulting injuries would have been enough to insure death.

"You died way too easy," Slocum grumbled. He stood, went and caught his frightened horse and returned to the dead man's side. The horse smelled blood and got spooked, so Slocum led it back to where he had staked it out earlier. By now, he was eager to find the map and see what had caused the death of two men.

Slocum dropped to his knees and fumbled open the man's coat. It took several minutes of searching before he found the leather case hidden away in a false pocket. Opening the wallet revealed a single sheet of paper. Slocum pulled it out and unfolded it, then frowned. There was only half a sheet here. He hunted through the rest of the wallet but couldn't find the part torn away.

A more thorough search failed to uncover the rest of the map.

Slocum closed his eyes and concentrated on remembering everything he had seen when this owlhoot had gunned down Preston at the saloon. To the best of his recollection, the half sheet was all he had stolen off Preston's body.

"Not much of a map," Slocum observed, turning it over and over in a vain attempt at orienting it. Not only couldn't he determine which way was north on the map, he found it hard to understand the crabbed legend or the X's that probably represented mountains. It was nowhere he had seen.

"This was worth a man's life?" He glared at the dead outlaw. He hardly included this life. The robber would have died sooner or later, by bullet or noose, but Preston was another matter. The saloon owner had family.

And Slocum had promised to get this scrap of paper to a brother in Virginia City. He shook his head at the task before him.

"Anything else?" he asked the dead man as he went through his pockets one last time. Slocum jerked back, his finger cut and bleeding. "What caused that?" He ripped open the dead man's shirt to expose a chain around the neck. Hanging on it was half a gold coin with the sharp edge that had drawn his blood.

Slocum jerked the chain off the dead neck and held up the coin. It was a tiny twenty-dollar gold piece that had been cut in half leaving a sawtooth edge. A scratch on the back was still bright and shiny but the front of the double eagle was . . . ordinary.

No one carried an ordinary coin around his neck as this man had. Or put away a scrap of paper into a special wallet as if it were the most valuable item in the world. Slocum was missing something important.

The only way he could find out what all this meant was to find Preston's brother and ask.

He set about burying the dead murderer, then rode deeper into the Sierras, until the last dying rays of sunlight vanished and plunged the trail into utter darkness. He pitched camp for the night and this time his dreams were of jagged gold coins and mysterious maps.

4

The storm had left the pass looking like a wonderland of white, with pines and spruce poking through to lend green accents along with the rusty brown and red rocks that reminded Slocum of the Rockies. He let his horse pick its way up the trail, and before he knew it, he was looking down a winding road on the far side of the pass. As he rode he thought and even fingered the curious map that had been stolen from Preston.

Most of all, he puzzled over the half gold coin. It had been meticulously cut in two, as if someone had used a jeweler's saw to produce the precise zigzag pattern. But stranger yet was the scratch. Slocum held it up so the sunlight glinted off the tiny coin and highlighted the scratch. From one deep cut it ran diagonally across the coin to a notch on the edge. As straight as it was, Slocum doubted it had been accidental. Slocum tucked it back into his pocket. Worrying about it did no good without more information. If nothing else, he had half of a double eagle to spend.

As his horse made a sharp turn in the road, he saw Virginia City stretched up and down the eastern side of Mount Davidson. He had been passing mines for some time and had skirted the road leading to Gold Hill, the town on the far side of the mountain from Virginia City. Slocum wanted to find Preston's brother quickly, give him the map and then move on. The storm had convinced him that he would be caught in the town if he waited until another roared down from the north. Winter was coming early this year, and Slocum had no reason to stay in a boomtown like Virginia City.

Slocum couldn't remember how many towns like this he had seen. Right now, with silver flowing from the Comstock Lode like water down the Mississippi, men crowded the narrow streets and filled them from side to side. Some were prospectors looking to make their fortune by finding the big strike, the mother lode, the draw hole that would make them richer than Leland Stanford or Collis Potter Huntington. Others held more realistic goals, looking only to work in established mines. Still others sold merchandise to the miners and mine owners.

The mine owners got richer by the day because of the backbreaking labor of the miners. But perhaps the best of all were those merchants selling the goods necessary to keep the boom flourishing. They provided a service that kept the town alive, made a decent profit and breathed clean air and stood in bright sun.

Where would he find Preston's brother?

Slocum tried counting saloons as he rode and gave up when he hit thirty, since he only rode on one street. Union Street below him on the mountainside looked to have as many, if not more than the one he was on. The brothels on Sutton Avenue were quiet now but would be doing a roaring business later, when the miners changed shifts. Asking questions in any of the houses of ill repute would get him nowhere. He would not bank on Preston's brother also being a barkeep, but he knew no other place to ask and hope to get a reply. Even in a saloon it was a dangerous pursuit, since miners and prospectors disliked anyone asking too many questions, but Slocum had faced worse challenges.

He flexed his hand. The leather glove cracked as he did so. Being trapped out in the storm probably had been more dangerous. Facing the killer in a shoot-out definitely was more dangerous than knocking back a shot of whiskey here and there in Virginia City while asking after Preston.

As he rode slowly through the throng, his sharp eyes moved from one side of the street to the other. For no good reason, he picked the Firehouse No. 7 Saloon to start. Slocum dismounted, stretched his tired muscles, then made sure his horse was close enough to a water trough to drink its fill. Before long he would find the stables and see to a nosebag of grain for the horse. It had served him well getting across the snowy fields and up steep mountain passes to arrive here.

"Here" was like any number of other saloons he had been in. The only thing that struck him as odd about the Firehouse No. 7 Saloon was the relative quiet for so many men—and the men were, for the most part, dressed similarly. They wore rubber coats with bright brass plates on the breast and many had military-looking leather helmets on the bar beside them. As he neared, Slocum saw that the men were all firemen.

"I'm new to town," he said to the barkeep, who eyed him critically. "Anyone mind if I have a drink or two here?"

"This here's reserved for volunteer firemen," the barkeep said, but he was obviously impressed that Slocum didn't bull his way in and had some recognition of social class. In most boomtowns, the firemen were at the top of the social heap. From the looks on these men's faces, Virginia City was one of them. With fire an ever-present danger to the flimsy buildings that had sprung up like mushrooms after a spring rain, those who risked their lives to save both property and lives were a cut above the norm. In addition, such fire departments accepted a prospective volunteer only after rigorous initiation.

"Thanks anyway," Slocum said, turning to go. From farther down the bar he heard whispers being exchanged among three of the men. Before he got to the door, one of the firemen called out to him.

"Hold your horses, mister. I'll stand you a round. Ain't often we get newcomers to Virginia City with manners."

"Much obliged," Slocum said. He saw that the man who had spoken wore a lieutenant's badge on his hat.

"You don't have the look of a miner about you," the fireman said. "Not a gambler, either, not like most of the damn tinhorn thieves coming here these days."

Slocum accepted the shot of whiskey, looked at it with anticipation, then downed it in a gulp. It was good liquor, not the cheap trade whiskey made with raw alcohol, gunpowder and rusty nails served in most mining towns.

"Good," he said, wiping his lips. "Could I buy you and your friends one?" These men might be the social upper crust in Virginia City, but they weren't above accepting a free drink. In a few minutes Slocum had made the acquaintance of the lieutenant and his two aides.

"Name's Sparky and these here gents are my good buddies Hugh Lawson and Big Ed Zelowski. Ain't his real name. Nobody's ever been able to pronounce it right, so that's his moniker."

"Ed," the huge man said, grinning and showing two missing front teeth. "It's Ed they can't pronounce." The men laughed at what had to have been a joke told a hundred times. Slocum joined in.

"You gents probably know everyone in town. I'm looking for a man named Preston." He watched their expressions change from joviality to caution.

"You some kind of bounty hunter?" asked Sparky. "We don't hold with them, not here, not in Company No. 7."

"I've got some bad news for him. Not looking to run him in."

"Bad news?" asked Lawson. "What might it be?"

"That's between me and him, when I find him. Let's just say I have an inheritance to pass along from his brother. You don't know anyone named Preston?" The trio was still chary to talk about any Virginia City inhabitant with a stranger, but Slocum guessed they didn't know Preston. To be certain, Slocum described Preston the best he could, but he might have been describing half the men in town. There was no rule requiring Preston's brother to look anything like him, either.

"Sorry we can't help you, Slocum," Sparky said. "Most of us don't get out of town much. We work in the Silver King Mine, when we're not servin' the community as firemen."

"Or gettin' soused right here at the ole No. 7!" cried Big Ed.

Slocum listened to them go on about the fires they had fought, how some were difficult and others easily extinguished. He made appropriate sounds and nodded occasionally to keep them talking, but got no further clue as to whether they knew Preston. Probably not, since there were so many newcomers to town. Not only were there prospectors and miners, but also lumbermen and freighters and scores of other professions necessary to support a town digging millions of dollars of silver from the ground. The smelter at the foot of Mount Davidson employed more than two hundred men, most all of them having come to Virginia City within the past few weeks. Slocum knew all this from what the firemen said in passing.

Finding Preston's brother seemed less promising by the minute.

"You certainly know how to throw a party," Slocum complimented, "but I have to get settled in. Any idea where I can find a room for the night?"

This produced a gale of laughter from the men. Sparky wiped his eyes and came away with streaks of gray dirt.

"Slocum, that's 'bout the funniest thing we heard in a spell. Ain't no hotel rooms in this danged place. A couple on the edge of town are bein' built, but no tellin' when they'll open. What rooms there are sleep a dozen men across—in each direction."

"Likely to charge more 'n you'd care to spend, too," chimed in Hugh Lawson. "That's why there's so many rickety buildings. Can't put 'em up fast enough for the folks blowin' into town." .

"I've slept under the stars before. No town ordinance against that, is there?"

"If there was, half the prospectors in Virginia City'd be in jail, which would solve their housing problems," said Sparky.

Slocum drank another round with the firemen, then drifted away as they got down to serious discussion of fighting fires. He reckoned it was better than listening to them talk about drilling, blasting and swinging pickaxes deep in the claustrophobic, boiling hot stope of a silver mine, but he wasn't sure.

As he stepped out on C Street, the cold wind whipping down from the elevation warned him of another Washoe Zephyr blowing in. He looked around and wondered how awful it might be staying here over the winter. Miners were notoriously bad gamblers, and he had plenty of money for a stake in any game likely to be held in a saloon along this street. Trying to pick the right time to leave between storms might get him frozen solid in some unexpectedly high pass if he guessed wrong.

"Not so bad," Slocum said as he walked along the street, glancing into saloons and dance halls. He saw plenty of soiled doves and even more miners willing to pay their price, whatever it might be. As he walked, however, a desolation settled on him. He might have looked square at the man he sought and not known it.

A particularly nasty-looking gambling establishment drew him. Slocum stood back, fended off the advances of the Cyprians plying their fleshy wares, and watched the miners gamble. A good faro game would make him a rich man before spring came back to the Sierras. Even splitting the take with the saloon owner, Slocum knew he could make thousands of dollars from the wild, ignorant way the miners bet. They were no different here than back in Truckee at the Stolen Nugget Saloon.

Slocum had to chuckle. He had briefly owned a saloon, and here he was thinking about gambling in another one.

"Hey, barkeep," he called. The man came over. "You know anybody named Preston?"

"Might. That's a common enough name. What's your business with him?"

"Got family business. His brother wanted me to give him something."

"Did he now?" the barkeep said, scowling darkly. "Don't know any Preston. And you might take your business elsewhere."

Slocum shrugged, finished his drink and went back outside. Darkness and considerable cold had wrapped Virginia City by now. Gaslights sputtered noisily along C Street and cast pale yellow light enough to read a newspaper by, if he had a newspaper. Slocum took two quick steps and jammed his spur down on a sheet of paper blowing past.

He had his newspaper. Scanning the *Territorial Enterprise* quickly showed him a listing of ads. If it came down to it, he could run a small ad asking after Preston's brother and offering a modest reward for that information. In a town of fabulous wealth, there was always crushing poverty. A five-dollar gold piece might go a long way toward loosening a tongue. Slocum tore out the masthead with the newspaper's address and tucked it into his coat pocket. Then he looked around, wondering where he might pitch his blanket for the night. Somewhere away from this main street.

He had seen a cemetery downhill before it had gotten too dark. Cemeteries were peaceful enough places to sleep.

Superstitious miners weren't likely to bother his sleep there, and Slocum was far removed from having any irrational awe of the dead. He had seen too many corpses to believe they ever came back.

He had put enough men into the ground to *know* they never came back.

Making his way back to where his horse waited impatiently, Slocum got the feeling of eyes following him. He turned and looked over his shoulder once but saw no one stand out in the crowd. The feeling had intensified by the time he mounted his horse and turned its face toward the road winding down toward the cemetery.

"Mr. Slocum," came a soft voice that filled the evening like a nightingale's song. A woman stepped from the deep shadows at the side of the Firehouse No. 7 Saloon. Slocum shielded the light from the nearby gaslight with his hand and studied her. At first he heard the soft whisper of her skirt hem across the boardwalk and the click of her shoes against the wood planking. She was dressed plainly, but what struck him most was her lack of a coat on such a chilly evening. She huddled forward a little, hands clutching her elbows in a vain attempt to hold in the heat.

His eyes worked up quickly to the heaving bosom and then to her face. A pale white oval, that face was about the loveliest he had seen in quite a while. She had the sophisticated air of the ladies in San Francisco but the edge of a frontierswoman. Her auburn hair flew about wildly as the wind whipped around the building. She appeared unaware of the hint of new snow on the air as she stared boldly, making Slocum feel he was the center of the universe.

"You have the advantage of me, ma'am," Slocum said, touching the brim of his hat. "You know my name."

"I'm Molly," she said, smiling prettily. "Molly Preston. I'm the sister of the man you're looking for."

"Do tell," Slocum said. "How is it Preston failed to mention having such a lovely sister?"

"Perhaps he didn't quite trust you, Mr. Slocum," she said. Then she laughed. "No, he trusted you completely if he sent you after Seamus."

Slocum nodded, absorbing information he had lacked. Preston had been Irish, judging from the faint brogue in his words. Having a brother named Seamus and a sister going by Molly fit well.

"Where can I find Seamus?" Slocum asked. The woman stepped closer, brushed a shock of hair from her eyes and looked up at him. He felt he could get mighty lost in this woman's bright blue eyes.

"He's not in town right now, but he ought to be back sometime tomorrow."

"I need to find a place to sleep tonight." Slocum turned up the collar of his coat as the wind took on a steel edge of a storm. "From the way the wind's blowing, I'd better go to earth pretty quick."

"Come on up to our place. Me and Seamus, we got a shack, it's not much, up on the side of Gold Hill. You're welcome to wait there for him."

Her bold gaze told Slocum more than her words.

"Lead the way. I'm not turning down such a charitable offer, not if I'd be out in the snow otherwise." He saw how she bit her lower lip, glanced down at her feet, then looked back at him almost shyly.

"I ain't got no horse or carriage. Could you see fit to let me ride?"

Slocum thrust out his left arm. Molly grabbed his hand and let him pull her up behind him in the saddle. She settled down quickly, her arms around his waist. He didn't put up any fuss when the woman's hands drifted down and rested over his crotch. The sensations moving into his loins as they rode grew until Slocum was about ready to explode by the time she had guided him up the steep side of the hill and along a narrow dirt path to a tumbledown shack.

"This your place?" he asked. Somehow, he reckoned a

woman as pretty as Molly would have a better place. Maybe not one like the millionaires down lower on the hill but better than this rickety line shack. But, he reminded himself, Virginia City was a boomtown and finding any shelter was hard. This might be the best she and her brother could manage. From her worn dress Slocum guessed Molly and Seamus didn't have a great deal of money.

That might change when he gave her brother the map.

"No matter how humble, there's no place like home," Molly said, releasing her grip around his waist and sliding lithely to the ground. She smoothed her skirts but the wind whipped them up, giving Slocum a quick look at the woman's ankles. She knew the effect she had on him. Molly flashed a quick grin that bordered on the lewd, then pushed the door open and went inside without a word.

Slocum saw a lean-to around back that served as a crude stable. He dismounted, led his horse to it, then made sure some hay was in a trough and that the horse had ample water. If it got too cold, the water would freeze, but not drinking would be the least of the horse's—or Slocum's—worries. Taking his gear, he went back to the door leading into the shack.

He stooped dead in his tracks in the doorway. For a second, he thought his eyes played tricks on him. Maybe a snowflake had fluttered in and temporarily blurred his sight. Or shadows cast by a flickering kerosene lamp playing through the room made him see what wasn't there.

"Come on in and shut the door. I'm getting' mighty chilly standin' here like this," said Molly.

"Do tell," Slocum said, dropping his saddle just inside the door. He took off his gloves and shucked out of his gunbelt, but he never took his eyes off Molly Preston. She was buck naked and lolled back on the cot stretched on the far side of the room.

The cold tightened her already firm breasts and made the feisty woman's nipples spring up hard and red atop the hills of snow-white flesh. Those succulent mounds might be snow white but they weren't cold, not like the snow beginning to fall faster outside. Slocum found that out quickly when he sat on the edge of the cot, bent low and sucked one of the nips into his mouth.

Molly gasped, sagged back and shoved her chest upward so he could better tend both of those tasty tidbits. Slocum obliged her by licking, sucking, kissing and then moving to the other nipple. As he worked to tongue the rubbery tips, her fingers frantically sought to free him of his clothing.

Slocum repositioned himself a little and let the woman work feverishly to get him as naked as she was. As she worked, he drew back and studied her. Molly's body was sleek and firm and damned near perfect. Her alabaster skin slipped like velvet under his exploring fingertips and then rippled in excited anticipation when he reached a sensitive spot on the inside of her thigh. Molly's legs parted of their own accord to reveal a coppery-colored nest of fur hiding the location where both wanted Slocum to explore further.

"Go on," she said. "I can tell you want to."

"If you keep working like that's a pump handle, you might just cause a gusher," Slocum said. The woman's hand had curled around his rigid manhood and worked up and down furiously. He slipped about on the narrow cot so she could hang onto his hard length but so he got an even better look at her naked beauty.

"You're the one," he said. Molly jerked back a little and looked at him with her bright blue eyes.

"What do you mean by that?" she asked.

"You're the one that got all the good looks in the Preston family," Slocum said. "Unless Seamus is one handsome galoot."

Molly laughed in delight.

"You are such a charmer, Mr. Slocum."

"John," he said, then shut off any further talk by locking

his lips against hers. The kiss deepened as their desires rose to match the wind howling louder and louder by the minute. Slocum's tongue probed out and dueled with Molly's. Hers slithered back and away and then swirled about his, stroking and racing to and fro until both were gasping for breath.

Then Slocum worked lower with his kisses, going to her chin, back to her closed eyes, all over her cheeks and ears and sleek, arching neck. Not content, he slipped lower to lavish more kisses on her firm breasts. The gooseflesh had vanished as her heart raced faster. Slocum nibbled first on one nipple and then the other, tasting the woman's salty sweat. He spiraled down one milky white cone of teat flesh, frolicked orally in the deep valley he found and finally worked his wet way up the other.

By the time he reached this summit, Molly thrashed about on the bed. She moved around, positioned herself and opened her legs widely so she could wrap them around his waist. Slocum was firmly held in place—as if he intended to go anywhere.

He lifted himself up enough to position himself at the gates of paradise.

Outside, it was a cold, wintry night. Inside, warmth enveloped him totally.

"Oh, yes, John, this is so good," Molly sobbed out. She clutched at his upper arms and then slid her fingers down and hunched up enough to reach behind and grab his muscular rump. She pulled hard to draw him even deeper into her moist, intimate recess. Slocum allowed her to guide him that extra inch.

For a few seconds he simply enjoyed the feel of such a hot, tight sheath of female flesh around his steely length. Then he began drawing back. Molly's sobs of protest momentarily sounded louder than the wind building outside. Then her shrieks of pure joy filled the cabin as Slocum rammed back and ground his crotch into hers, stirring his rigid pole about like a spoon in a mixing bowl. The woman began twitching and bucking like a bronco. Slocum rode her well.

Her knees pulled back until they were on either side of Slocum's body. With a quick swoop down, he got one of his arms under her knee and lifted. This drove him into her at a different angle, giving both of them new thrills of carnal pleasure. When lightning bolts began surging up and down his length as he stroked powerfully, Slocum had to slow. He wanted this to last all night. But the woman wasn't going to let it.

She reached down between them and found the dangling hairy sac. Molly began squeezing it, teasing it, giving him sensations he had seldom felt before. Slocum leaned forward as he stroked inward, bending her knee back toward her chest. Her other leg curled about his waist to attempt the impossible task of pulling him even closer, even deeper.

Slocum felt the woman trembling constantly, as if she had been thrust out into the storm. But the sex sweat beading her face and body belied that. He knew she was close to exploding in lust. He altered his pace and began moving with short, quick strokes guaranteed to excite Molly the most. And they did.

She gasped, arched her back and lifted her hindquarters off the bed, and then vented a cry of pure ecstasy. As she cried out, the tightness surrounding Slocum's hidden length compressed even more, squeezing him flat.

This was more than he could tolerate. His careful rhythm vanished as he flashed back and forth, driving his meaty stake deep into her needy well. The heat mounted inside his loins, spread like wildfire and then exploded outward in a fiery rush that left him drained.

He sank beside Molly on the cot and drew her close. She shivered and snuggled so she could bury her face in his shoulder.

"You're good, John. Maybe too good."

"I had some powerful inspiration," he said. "And how can I be too good?"

Molly mumbled something, pulled the thin blanket up over their naked, intertwined bodies and settled down. In a few minutes she was sound asleep. Slocum lay awake for a while listening to the fierce howl of the autumn storm blowing down along Mount Davidson and covering Virginia City with a new coating of snow.

It was freezing outside but as hot as he could handle in the tiny shack. He fell asleep thinking it might be just fine spending the winter in Virginia City.

5

The screech of the wind died down a few hours before dawn. Slocum turned on the narrow cot and then opened his eyes when he didn't feel the woman's naked warmth against him. He scooted up a little in the bed to get a better look across the room to where Molly crouched by his gear. The bright light shining off the newly fallen snow outside lit up the inside of the shack better than any kerosene lamp ever could. Slocum clearly saw how the woman went through every item in his saddlebags, then carefully repacked them and moved on to check the pockets in his clothing.

"How much?" Slocum asked. Molly jumped as if she had been stuck with a pin.

"Wh-what do you mean?" she asked. She turned, not trying to hide her pert breasts or the furry triangle nestled between her thighs. Slocum knew she wanted him distracted from what he had just seen. It almost worked. Molly was a mighty pretty filly.

"Whores collect their due from the men they roll around with in the sack," he said. "How much do you charge?"

"Oh, John, it's not like that. Not at all. I . . . I was just—"

43

"Trying to rob me," he finished in a cold, level tone. Slocum swung his legs off the bed. The frigid air hit him like a sledgehammer. He quickly dressed, but the clothing had been laying out all night and was partly frozen. It took a bit of moving around to break the ice off his jeans and get his shirt on.

"I wasn't doin' anything of the sort," she said primly. "I was just tryin' to help you out. You got a map to give my brother. I was goin' take it so I could give it to Seamus myself. That'd save you the trouble."

"When did I mention any map?" Slocum began to wonder how many people knew of Preston's map—and what it meant.

"That's why you're in Virginia City, ain't it? To give Seamus our brother's map?"

"I'll pass it over to him personally. That's mighty thoughtful of you to want to take on my sworn duty, but I'm not like that," Slocum said mockingly.

"Oh, John, I *know* how you are. You're a magnificent stud!" She came to him and pressed herself against him hard enough to flatten her breasts. Then she moved in small, beguiling circles that rubbed her body all over his chest. Slocum returned her kisses without much enthusiasm. He was beginning to wonder if he ought to spend any more time in Virginia City than necessary to see that Preston's map was given to its proper owner.

"When might Seamus be back?" Slocum asked.

"I can't say. He's up in the mountains workin' a claim. With this much snow, he might be days and days."

Slocum went to the door and tugged on it a few seconds before it opened. The snow had drifted less than knee-high. On the flat, only an inch had fallen. The wind had been fierce, but it was still too early in the season for a significant snowfall.

"If you know where he is, tell me and I'll ride out so he won't have to be bothered."

"I, uh, of course, John," Molly said. She gathered her clothing strewn around the tiny cabin and began dressing. In spite of himself, Slocum appreciated the sight of all that sleek white skin slowly vanishing behind her frilly undergarments and then all disappearing behind her heavier dress. She knew he watched, and she made dressing into a show, thinking that would further bring him under her thumb.

She didn't know John Slocum.

"Fix some food, if there is any," Slocum said. "I can hunt a rabbit, but that'll take a spell. This late in the fall, the rabbits are mighty skittish about getting out of their burrows in the snow. They haven't had a chance to change coloration from brown to white."

"Oh, there's plenty to eat around here," Molly said, turning around and searching as if she had no idea what might be in the meager larder. She rummaged about in an old dynamite case and fished out a solitary tin plate and some canned goods. She looked up and smiled. "Hope you don't mind canned tomatoes and peaches for breakfast. That's 'bout all I got here."

"I've eaten worse," Slocum said.

"Have you now?" she said, grinning. "Tell me about it while we chow down."

Slocum found himself spinning wild tales that had nothing to do with his actual experiences. Something about Molly was beginning to turn him wary. But she was one fine-looking woman, and that eased a considerable amount of the uneasiness.

After they had eaten, sharing off the single tin plate, he went outside and tended his horse. The animal had fared well in the lean-to. The shed was out of the wind and the water in the trough hadn't even frozen all the way. The horse had poked holes in the icy crust with its nose and had continued to drink during the night. But the horse needed more hay, which Slocum gave from a small pile under a tarp.

He led his saddled horse back around to the front of the shack. Molly was gone.

"Don't that beat all?" he muttered. Her footprints in the snow led downhill toward Virginia City. If he wanted to track her, he could have done it with his eyes shut. This caused him to frown. The woman had to know that, since she had made no effort to hide her path. He wasn't going to find Seamus Preston without her help, not if the miner was hidden away in the valleys and ravines meandering throughout the mountains. Some of the canyons were downright treacherous and others hard to find. Those were the ones most prized by prospectors since others might have missed them and left the mother lode undiscovered.

Slocum went into the shack and boiled himself some coffee. A quick check showed that the map still resided in his coat pocket where he had put it. He touched his shirt pocket and outlined the sawed-up gold piece. On impulse, he took it out and used the leather thong running through a tiny hole in the piece to make a necklace for himself. The cold coin dropped against his skin and warmed immediately, safely out of sight.

As he drank his coffee, he thought on his night with Molly. Before he could come to any conclusions, he heard the steady clop of approaching hoofbeats. Slocum swallowed the rest of his coffee, stashed the cup in his saddlebags and walked around his horse to see Molly riding carefully up the trail toward the cabin.

"I had to fetch my horse."

"You left your horse in town all night?" Slocum asked, shaking his head. "Why didn't you ride him up here then?" He distinctly remembered her saying she didn't have a horse, but he didn't remark on this lie.

"The way we came was more fun," she said, giving him her impish grin. "Come on now. We got miles to ride if we want to get to Seamus 'fore the sun sets."

"It's that far?" Slocum gauged the time from the sun rising to the east, then checked his pocket watch.

"Not so far, but I reckon we can find reasons to take quite a few breaks along the trail," Molly said. She laughed, sawed on her reins to get her horse turned and headed upslope. With a wild rake of her heels, she set the horse to trotting away from the shack. Slocum wondered what he was getting into, but he mounted and followed at a more cautious pace. The rocky trail was slippery with ice and snow, and being stranded because the horse broke a leg was the last thing Slocum wanted.

Slocum let the woman take the lead but watched her carefully. From the way she paused at various forks in the road, he wondered if she had any idea where her brother worked that claim. Too much didn't ring true, but Slocum couldn't complain much. It had been a good way to spend the night, Molly curled up next to him during the worst of the storm.

The sun finally poked above the mountain peaks and began melting the snow, turning dirt into cold, clinging mud.

"How long you and Seamus been in Virginia City?" Slocum asked when they halted for a noonday meal. They had to eat from Slocum's larder since Molly had nothing in her saddlebags.

"Oh, a while. Who keeps track of time?" she asked.

"Tell me about your brother." Slocum watched her closely.

"Seamus is quite the worker. Always out in the hills, pokin' into the rock—"

"Not Seamus. Your other brother." Slocum rested his hand over the coat pocket holding the map Preston had wanted him to deliver. The blood on this half sheet of paper was beginning to wear on Slocum. It had been worth killing Preston for, and the outlaw who had murdered him had gone to his grave for it.

"I got a lot of other brothers," she said, her blue eyes fixed intently on Slocum. She knew what he meant but danced around answering. Maybe because she couldn't. Slocum let the matter drop and turned to his plate of beans and bacon. Molly's evasiveness bothered him but he got a sense of danger building from some other quarter.

"You know, John, you're actin' mighty strange today. What's wrong? It's not me, now is it?" Molly demanded. "Is it somethin' I did—or somethin' I didn't do and you wanted me to?"

Slocum cleaned his tin plate and returned it to his saddlebags without answering. He looked down the canyon where they had spent a good part of the morning making their way up the steep trail.

"You know them?" he asked.

"Who are you talkin' 'bout?" Molly asked. She jumped to her feet and followed Slocum's gaze. "Damnation! We got road agents on our tail."

Slocum guessed many men had been on Molly's tail, but that wasn't his concern. He watched as the dark figures moved past an unmelted snowfield, counting softly to himself. Eight. That number ruled out prospectors. Those were solitary characters, sometimes with a partner, usually willing to tough it out hunting long weary hours by themselves. It might be lonely, but if they hit it big, there wasn't anybody to share it with. Or so they thought.

These weren't prospectors.

Slocum guessed they weren't miners on their way to a dig, either, by the way they occasionally stopped and studied the ground. Slocum had made no effort to hide their tracks since they had followed the narrow trail. Even if he had tried to cover the hoofprints, it would have been time-consuming and difficult since they were the first travelers to come this way since the snowfall. Dirt could be smoothed over. Repairing hoofprints in snow was nigh on impossible, though he had heard how the Nez Perce did it to confuse their enemies.

"Do you know who they might be?" he asked.

"I . . . I don't know who they are. Just men out on the trail," Molly said without conviction.

"Where does this trail lead?" Slocum asked. He looked into the mountains and knew there wasn't a pass here. Geiger Pass to Reno was to their north. The train from Gold Hill had laid its tracks some ways south. Not casual pilgrims, not railroad men, certainly not prospectors in such a pack—that didn't leave much else but road agents working this trail, hunting for prospectors taking nuggets back to Virginia City for assay.

"Could be claim jumpers," Slocum guessed. If that were true, he and Molly had nothing to fear. Slocum didn't believe it for an instant. These men studied the trail—the trail he and Molly had left. It didn't take much for him to figure out they wanted the map riding easy in his coat pocket.

"You don't know what kind of animals prowl these here mountains," Molly said uneasily. "We ought to be sure they don't find us."

Her obvious nervousness told him she wasn't in league with them but that she knew them.

"Which way is your brother's claim?" Slocum asked. "It would be a good idea to head some other way, at least for a while."

"There, no there," Molly said, flustered. She kept looking downhill where the riders appeared and disappeared between high boulders bordering the trail. She turned and pointed to the right. "We can go up into that there branchin' canyon and hide, leastways till they're gone." The auburn-haired beauty watched their backtrail more than she looked ahead where she had suggested they take cover.

Slocum didn't bother telling her that there was no way

to sneak off without the eight men knowing right away. The snow was turning to mud in the warm autumn sun, but they had to cross too many patches of snow to avoid leaving a trail a blind man could follow. Slocum jumped to the top of the largest boulder and studied the terrain where they had to go, if they sought refuge in that canyon. As far as Slocum could tell, it was as good as any other hidey-hole and had the advantage of being closer than other canyons meandering off into the higher mountains.

"We can throw them off the trail for a hundred yards," he said, jumping down. "Follow me as close as possible."

He settled his saddlebags so they rode easy on the horse's hindquarters, checked to be sure his spare Colt Navy stashed there was loaded and ready, then swung into the saddle. Slocum walked his horse slowly across a rocky stretch, then kept to the patches of thick mud as much as possible. He kept his eyes straight ahead, figuring Molly would follow as well as she could.

"John," she said in a choked voice, "are they gonna catch us?"

"Not if I can help it. Keep quiet. Voices carry in the mountains." What he said was true, but Slocum also wanted to concentrate on picking his path carefully. Another hundred yards brought him to a snowy patch that could not be avoided. He chose parts of the snow where shadows were cast by the rocks higher on the trail. These would vanish as the sun sank low in the west, but the geography was on Slocum's side. Twilight came fast because of the high mountains they rode into.

"John, what if they do catch us?"

Slocum glared at her. There would be a fight somewhere along the way, and he did not want Molly griping constantly. He needed to direct his full effort toward the difficult task of getting the hell away from the riders. Unlike the woman, he didn't need to look at their backtrail to know the men were coming on like some inexorable force of nature.

He had delayed the road agents by a few minutes, if luck was with him. They had to find a place to make a stand if they couldn't outleg the men.

He saw it a ways down the canyon to their right. The steep cliffs were too sheer for him to hope to reach the rim before the men on their tail spotted them. There were probably several trails chiseled in the rocky walls that would allow them to reach safety above, but he had no time to find them.

"There," Slocum said. "That mine."

"I don't see any mine—oh, there," Molly said, squinting as she spotted what he had already seen. "That can be dangerous, going into an abandoned mine."

"Most were left because there wasn't any silver inside, not because they were going to collapse," Slocum said. If a miner thought there was even a single ounce of gold or silver remaining in a hillside, he would reopen even the most dangerous mine shaft with his bare hands.

"We kin ride real fast and get out the other end of the canyon," Molly said. She chewed her lower lip and looked about desperately, like a trapped animal.

"Don't think there is another end to this canyon. From the way it just stops ahead, it's a box canyon."

"What? You led us into a trap!"

Slocum restrained himself. She had been the one who had pointed out this canyon as a refuge. He began to think Molly had no notion where Seamus Preston worked his claim and had never ridden this way before today. If he wanted to be sure of his own safety, he ought to leave her behind. He ought to but couldn't.

"We ride into the mine and stay quiet, they might think we've found a way out of the box," Slocum said. "If nothing else, they'll have a harder time finding us." He looked

down and saw they had left the snowy patch they had ridden through and were again on solid rock that didn't take
kindly to hoofprints. As a tracker, Slocum hated terrain
like this. As a man trying to get away from road agents on
his trail, he found it a godsend.

"This way," he ordered, choosing his route to the mouth
of the mine carefully. He kept to rocky areas and those
where hooves wouldn't dig betraying marks into the snow.
When they were within a few yards of the mine, he slid to
the ground and urged his balky horse forward into the dark
mouth. Molly followed without saying a word to him, but
he heard her cursing under her breath like a wrangler
caught on barbed wire.

Slocum silently handed her the reins of his horse and
motioned her deeper into the mine. He pulled out his rifle
and crouched down just inside the mouth so he could watch
for riders.

Twenty minutes passed before he breathed a little easier.

"Well?" Molly demanded.

"I think they rode past us. We can get out of here and
leave them wandering around in a box canyon for a spell."

The words had hardly left his lips when he spotted a
road agent slowly approaching, eyes intent on the ground
as he followed their faint tracks. Trapped!

6

"Do you know him?" asked Slocum as he fingered his rifle. It was an easy shot, but taking out this lone rider would bring the rest of the gang down on their necks.

"Never seen him before," Molly said. Slocum looked at her sharply. Her eyes were wide, and she appeared the soul of innocence. He didn't have to be much of a poker player to know she was lying like a rug. "Well, I haven't," she went on. "I don't know who them gents are. But they don't mean us no good. You can tell by the way they're doggin' our tracks."

Slocum knew they weren't out on the trail for their health. The men had the hard look of killers to him. Who else rode in such a big band? He touched his pocket to assure himself that Preston's map was still there. Molly wanted it badly. Unless he missed his guess, these eight did, too. How did they know he had it?

Slocum looked again at the woman and decided she was the cause of most of his woe. From the frightened expression on her face, she and the men down the slope weren't in cahoots—far from it. With all the interest in what had to be the map, Slocum wondered if it really was valuable. He shrugged that off. Not only did he have to get out of a tight fix right now, but also it wasn't his map. It belonged to Preston's brother. If that was Seamus Preston, then Seamus could deal with the map and all the problems it brought with it. Slocum wasn't going to renege on a promise made to a dying man.

"Stay out of sight, no matter what happens," Slocum said.

"What are you gonna do, John?"

He ignored her, rested his rifle against the rocky wall of the mine shaft and slipped into the night. The darkness had cloaked them before and now gave him the chance he needed to work closer to the man sniffing their way by the minute. Slocum crawled onto a pile of mine tailings and waited. The man looked up just as Slocum launched himself through the air.

Crashing hard into the man carried both of them over the back of the horse onto the ground. Slocum kept twisting and had the advantage of surprise working for him as he landed hard on top of the man. For an instant he thought the man would fight. Then all the air and strength gusted from him. Slocum reared back, looked down and saw the glazed eyes, flaring nostrils and gaping mouth. He judged his distance and swung, connecting squarely on the man's jaw to put him out like a light. Slocum cursed the way the blow smarted and how his knuckles had been skinned, but he had been forced to act quickly.

"Get his horse. Don't let it run off," Slocum called to Molly. To his surprise, she acted right away and grabbed the trailing reins before the horse had gone a dozen feet.

"You kill the son of a bitch?" she asked.

"Are you sure you don't know him?"

"Mighta seen him around. Don't recall. I'm mad because he was followin' us like he was. No call for a man to do that, scarin' a woman out of a year's growth."

Slocum quickly searched the man's pockets but found nothing but a half dozen five-dollar gold pieces. That was a powerful lot for a cowpoke to be carrying, but from the look of the fallen man, he was no wrangler. Slocum's first impression had been right: road agent.

"Let me get him tied up," Slocum said, rolling the man onto his belly. He thrust the man's worn six-shooter into his own belt and completed the task of hog-tying him by using nearby rusty wire.

"Just kill him," Molly said. "Why leave him alive?"

"You want to cut his throat?" Slocum asked. He saw that Molly wouldn't find that out of the question. "Never mind. Gag him. He's not going to bother us any more."

"What are we gonna do? The rest of 'em are still out there," she said.

Slocum wondered if he might eliminate the opposition one by one, but he had been lucky this time. If there had been a second man, he would have been forced to shoot both of them, bringing the rest down on him like a flock of buzzards onto a fresh carcass. He went to a pile covered by a tarp nearby and pulled the canvas back.

"What'd you find?"

"Dynamite. A case of it. Old, too." Slocum looked around and wondered how long the mine had been abandoned. A year or more? Any explosive left outside that long would be unstable as hell and might blow up in his face if he even touched the crate.

Slocum pried off the flimsy wooden top and peered inside. Even as dark as it was, he saw the yellow ooze beaded all around the red-paper-wrapped sticks of dynamite. The nitroglycerin in each stick had seeped out, turning this crate into instant death.

"What are you gonna do?"

"Get all the horses—take the one we just acquired off our unwanted guest—and get ready to ride. If I set off a big enough blast, I can bring down a chunk of rock that will block the mouth of the canyon."

"You'd trap us!" Molly exclaimed.

"Don't have much choice. If the dynamite sticks had been new, I might have figured out a way of using them against the seven still on our trail. I need to distract them from wondering what's happened to their partner." Slocum jerked his thumb in the direction of the bound and gagged man.

"We can still kill him," Molly said, frowning mightily. "Why not kill him if we're gonna kill the others?"

Slocum wasn't sure he could come close to blowing up the others. He had one chance with the dynamite, and it was risky.

"Get mounted and get ready."

"Into the canyon?" she asked. Her skepticism was obvious.

"We might lure them deeper into the canyon, circle back, then set off the blast and trap them," Slocum said. He doubted it was possible and figured that the gang was spread out from one side to the other hunting for them. The one who had been tied up had been unlucky enough to find them.

"All right," Molly said, warming to the notion. "We get out of this and I'll make sure you get somethin' special, John. Real special."

"First things first," Slocum said as he gingerly lifted the case of dynamite. If a sharp movement disturbed the leaky sticks, he was a goner. Walking slowly past the pile of tailings, he found the spot he remembered from when they had ridden to the mine. The rock outcropping stretched up halfway to the canyon rim. He hoped an explosion here wouldn't cause other mines to collapse, but he had seen no other activity in the canyon.

"That's gonna bring down a powerful lot of rock," Molly said, looking up into the night. Stars outlined the rim. "How're you gonna set it off?"

For that Slocum didn't have a good answer. A sharp jolt

might do the trick, but he preferred to use miner's fuse—
which he didn't have.

He had started to look for some when he heard hooves
clicking against rock as at least two riders made their way
uphill to the mine.

"We've got more company," he said. Slocum carefully
put heavy rocks on top of the crate, leaving the side exposed. He went to his horse, drew the Winchester from the
sheath and pointed into the canyon.

"I don't wanna be caught," Molly whined.

"Get riding. Take my horse, too, and stop a quarter mile
off back out of the canyon. I'll join up with you in a few
minutes."

Molly didn't have to be told twice to get the hell away.
She clutched the reins on the other two horses and rode off
as fast as she could. Slocum heard the reaction of the approaching riders. They picked up the pace, leaving him no
choice.

Scrambling to find a good spot, Slocum ran a dozen
yards off before the first rider spotted him. The road agent
greeted him with repeated shots from his six-gun. Slocum
swung about, pulled the rifle in to his shoulder and fired.
His first round missed the crate and went whining off into
the night. His second hit the dynamite square on. For a moment he thought nothing was going to happen. Then a giant
windstorm lifted him, threw him back and sent him rolling
down the hill.

Somewhere along the way he lost the Winchester, but
the pain was so intense in his arms and face he hardly noticed. He had rolled through a big patch of prickly pear
cactus. Eventually he came to a halt and then was pelted
with rocks from above. Most were smaller stones but one
grazed his forehead and knocked him back. Then the world
turned entirely black, as a cloud of choking dust washed
over him. Rolling to his belly, Slocum curled up and let the

shock wave pass over him. He wondered vaguely how the dust and rock had preceded the sound, and then he was completely buried in a new rain of stone.

For what seemed an eternity Slocum lay on the ground. It took a while before he realized he could move. Pushing to his feet, he felt as if he was risen from the grave. Dust and pebbles fell off him, forcing him to draw up his bandanna to cover his mouth and nose.

"John! Over here, John!"

Staggering like a drunk, he made his way toward the voice in the dark. Before he had gone ten paces, he saw Molly astride a horse, looking down at him with some concern.

"Are you all right?" she asked. "You look a fright."

"I've felt better," Slocum admitted. He pulled himself into the saddle and for the first time got a sense of the havoc he had brought down. A quarter of the mountainside had collapsed like rotted wood and tumbled out into the canyon. If any of the men on their trail had been near the mine, they were dead. Slocum heaved a sigh of relief. He had almost been a goner. Only pure luck had sent the torrential downpour of rock away from him. As it was, he had been buffeted and pummeled within an inch of his life.

"We won't be getting out that way," he said. The rockfall had blocked them off from escape through the canyon mouth. They were trapped in a box canyon along with the road agents—the ones who had survived the avalanche. "Do you know any trails up to the rim?"

Molly shrugged. Again, Slocum got the feeling she was as new to this part of the country as he was and had no idea where to go. They set off to explore in silence, Slocum's watering eyes slowly getting the dust washed out of them. By midnight he had found a narrow trail with dozens of switchbacks leading to the rim, and by dawn they were back in Virginia City.

•   •   •

Slocum and Molly rode slowly down C Street. The town was stirring but not yet awake. Slocum spotted Sparky sitting on the doorstep of the Firehouse No. 7 Saloon and waved to him.

"Hey, Slocum. Thought you'd moved on," Sparky said, getting to his feet. From the way he grimaced, he was in big pain and needed the anesthetic offered by the bottle.

"Is there a marshal in town yet?" Slocum asked, remembering the fireman spinning a story about Virginia City losing its last one to the lure of the Comstock Lode.

Sparky laughed until tears ran down his dirty cheeks. He wiped at them with a large red polka-dot bandanna, then blew his nose.

"Sorry, Slocum. We go through marshals faster 'n most folks change their underwear."

"Those that have any underwear," Slocum said. "Is there any lawman down the street in the marshal's office?"

"Nope, not even a deputy. But heard tell the county sheriff was comin' into town. That'd be Sheriff George. Mean son of a buck, he is. Ain't never set eyes on him myself."

"About time someone in town did," Slocum said.

Sparky eyed the saddled spare horse, Molly and finally Slocum's disheveled condition.

"You been up to no good, Slocum?"

"Got to ask some questions of the law and find out about road agents," Slocum said.

"You got the look of a gent what's been pulled through a knothole backwards. But you, dearie, you look real fine." Sparky winked at Molly, who sniffed and pointedly turned away. Slocum looked from the fireman to Molly and frowned. If she and her brother had been around town long enough to stake out a claim, the lieutenant for a volunteer fire engine company ought to know her. Molly was a handsome enough looking woman to turn heads and get her image burned into even the most alcohol-besotted brain.

Slocum rode down the street and began dodging the increased foot traffic. By the time he reached the marshal's office, he was tired of so many people.

"Come on in and we'll tell the sheriff what happened," Slocum said. He saw that the woman dismounted and came along reluctantly. When they reached the door, Molly finally balked.

"You go. There's nothin' I can tell him."

"You got a good look at the road agents. He'll want you to confirm what I have to say."

"And what are you gonna say, John?" she asked. "That we upped and killed a half dozen folks who was ridin' along behind us? You do what you have to. I got business."

Slocum started to grab her arm, but the door to the hoosegow opened and a man filled it from side to side. The sheriff's badge on his vest told Slocum he had to deal with the law right away.

"What y'all goin' on about?" demanded the lawman. "I got me trouble a'plenty. Don't need—or want—more."

"You got more," Slocum said. He saw Molly sidle away out of the corner of his eye, then disappear around the side of the jailhouse. "I was riding west of town and eight men came after me."

"How do you mean 'came after me'?" Sheriff George looked as if he had bitten into something sour.

Slocum told of being followed and how the dynamite had gone off when the men started shooting. That was a stretch, but it saved him the explanation of how the riders hadn't actually done either him or Molly any harm before the explosion had buried them.

"So you don't rightly know what happened to any of them varmints?" The sheriff stroked his mustaches and skewered Slocum with his polar blue eyes.

Slocum shook his head.

"If you'd got a better look at 'em, I'd've been happier. Might be a gang of owlhoots I been after nigh on a month."

"Road agents?"

"That, high-graders, swindlers, 'bout anythin' crooked you can think up and some you probably can't." Sheriff George eyed Slocum even harder, then laughed. "I take back that last comment. You probably could think up most all their illegalities."

Slocum tensed. He had dodged a WANTED poster for killing a federal judge back in Georgia since the end of the war. More than this, he had done his share of what the sheriff called "illegalities."

"What makes you say that?"

Sheriff George laughed and slapped him on the back.

"Why, nothing, nothing a'tall. You have the look of a smart fellow who's been around. You musta seen it all and heard it all."

In spite of the lawman's bonhomie, Slocum felt like a bloody haunch being gnawed on by a coyote.

"You know them? The road agents?"

"Could be the gang I'm huntin' for," the sheriff said. "From what you say, that's Liberty Bell Canyon where they set off that dynamite. Might take a little ride out and look it over, just to be sure."

"Just to be sure," Slocum echoed.

"Have our paths crossed?" the sheriff asked unexpectedly. "Naw, reckon not. I'd've remembered, wouldn't I?"

Sheriff George went off, whistling tunelessly. Slocum watched until the lawman vanished down C Street, quickly lost in the throng filling the street now. He wondered at the way the sheriff had acted. Then he shrugged it off. It wasn't any concern of his. If Sheriff George had recognized him from a WANTED poster, there were plenty of cells inside the jailhouse that could take a new prisoner.

Slocum looked around and wondered what to do now. He still had Preston's map but was no closer to finding his brother.

7

Slocum found himself wondering what to do. He was beset by a gang of unknown road agents, for no reason he could tell, unless it had to do with the map. He suspected Molly knew more than she was telling. The lovely auburn-haired woman had hightailed it when he had told her he wanted to report everything that had happened to the sheriff. Looking around Virginia City, Slocum tried to locate her, but she had disappeared like smoke in a high wind.

Hitching up his gunbelt, Slocum retraced his path to the Firehouse No. 7 Saloon and climbed the steps. As he stepped inside, he was pushed back by a blast of hot air gusting from inside the saloon. It was getting mighty chilly outside, even during the day, but this was outrageously hot. Slocum looked over the swinging doors and saw a fire blazing merrily in the middle of the floor.

"Fire!" He pushed through and looked around for something to put out the flaming boards. If a fire took hold in a town with such rickety wood buildings, the town could vanish in a few minutes.

"Hold yer horses, Slocum," came the loud cry. Mingled with the words was a tad of laughter—at Slocum's expense. He looked around and saw all the firemen watching the fire. They wore their bright red shirts and had leather helmets with brass identification plates bright and shiny tucked under their arms.

"What's going on, Sparky?" Slocum entered and let the doors swing behind him. His front was sizzling hot from the fire while his other half still tingled with the cold of the autumn day.

"Jist a mite of in-struct-shun," the fireman said, coming over. He put his arm around Slocum's shoulders and guided him away from the fire. Slocum saw that the floor-boards weren't on fire. They had been pulled back to reveal a pit lined with red brick. The fire blazed merrily in it, but the smoke was filling the room to the point Slocum's eyes watered and he began to cough.

"Why'd you start it?" Slocum looked around and saw that the firemen were similarly afflicted. Not a one made a move to mop at his tears or use a dampened rag to cover mouth and nose to ease breathing. They suffered in silence.

"Test fer the newcomers. We got a couple inductees into Engine Company No. 7. You kin leave or watch."

Slocum squinted against the tears and brushed them away. At the far end of the bar one of the recruits began to totter. He took a step, dropped to one knee and tried to get up. Then he keeled over like he had been coldcocked. Two veterans hastily grabbed him under the arms and dragged him the length of the saloon to the jeers of the others.

The other recruit was made of sterner stuff. When he toppled, he did it like a buck private standing rigidly at attention too long in the hot sun. He hit the floor with a tremendous thud.

"Git 'im, men," shouted Sparky. "We got ourselves two blooded members of Engine Company No. 7!" A cheer went up. Then the men looked expectantly at their lieu-tenant. Sparky lifted his hand, then lowered it fast. The men closest to the fire began pissing on the blaze until it sizzled and popped.

"Come on. Do it right," urged Sparky. "Yer pissin' like a bunch o' old men!"

"Show us," demanded another fireman.

"You want to help out, Slocum? Not that I need it, mind you." Sparky motioned imperiously, and the barkeep brought over four large steins of beer. Sparky hefted one and downed it to the cheers of his company. Slocum figured there wasn't any reason not to join the fun. He matched the fireman drop for drop. Then they polished off the second stein and stepped up to the fire, now sizzling and popping but not yet extinguished. Slocum unbuttoned his fly and let loose his stream about the same time as the volunteer fireman.

"More beer! How kin a man do his duty without enough beer?" Both Sparky and Slocum were handed new steins. Never stopping their firefighting, they downed these. By the time the last drop had passed Slocum's lips, he ran dry.

But the fire was out.

"A dagnabbed tie, I'd say," said Sparky. "You're a good man, Slocum. Sure you don't want to try out for the company? Not a man here can match me, but you came danged close."

"Better," Slocum said, accepting another glass of beer.

"What's that?" roared Sparky.

"I said, I did better."

"Then you got to be put up for membership. No other company in Virginia City kin have a man better 'n the lieutenant of the best damned engine company in Nevada Territory!" The resulting cheer from Sparky's words spread like the very wildfire the men were entrusted with stopping.

Slocum wanted to get on with his chore of finding Preston's brother and delivering the map, but he found himself caught up in the firemen's high jinks. They were a cheerful bunch, and he wasn't going to insult them by turning down their invitation to join the engine company. Slocum had seen how status in this boomtown was determined—being a volunteer fireman ranked higher than about anything else, including mine foreman or millionaire.

"You done showed you could withstand heat and smoke, and you know the *best* way of puttin' out fires," Sparky said. "That leaves nothin' but the vote. Bring the jar and balls, my good man!" Sparky motioned to the barkeep, who scrounged around under the long bar until he found a large ceramic pot and two saucers filled with black and white balls.

Slocum had seen this kind of vote before for less palatable organizations. Every member of the engine company had a single vote. A white marble meant a vote for him. A lone black marble ended his chances of being a full-fledged member of Engine Company No. 7, and all the privileges that went with it in Virginia City. He stood by as the men each took a white and black ball, then put one secretly into the pot. For Slocum the outcome mattered less than it did for any of the men. They lived in Virginia City. He intended to be gone as soon as he could, in spite of it looking like a good place to ride out the winter.

His thoughts drifted to Molly and the problem she posed. Mostly, he knew better than to deal with such a dilemma before getting rid of the map and his duty to Preston.

"Here goes, Slocum," Sparky said loudly. The men had completed their vote. The lieutenant picked up the pot and held it over his head. He pulled out the marbles one by one. Each was white. As he counted out the final one, a huge cheer went up.

"You're one of us now, Slocum. One for all, all for one!" Sparky put the pot onto the bar and then turned, fixing Slocum with a gimlet stare. He said sternly, "There's one last ritual we gotta do."

"Before that," Slocum said, knowing what was coming, "let me buy the entire company a drink."

Sparky laughed as the barkeep pulled out a bottle and started pouring.

"You *are* one of us, Slocum. That was the last thing ya had to do."

Slocum drank with the men until almost eight o'clock. One by one, the men drifted off. Many were late for work. Others worked midnight shifts in the mines. But all were pleased at the addition to their fire engine company.

"Got to see to the equipment," Sparky said. "You gotta get a lesson on it, Slocum."

"Got my own job to do," Slocum said. He ran his finger around the rim of the shot glass and licked off the final drop of whiskey before asking, "You ever see the lady I rode into town with?"

"Woulda remembered a looker like her, Slocum. You know how to pick 'em. She your woman?"

Slocum shook his head. "Don't know who she belongs to. Maybe herself."

"Then she'll be workin' at Lil's or maybe Madame Mustache's place down on Sutton Avenue. She'd bring in a tidy sum for any cathouse." Sparky stopped, as if he might have offended Slocum hinting that Molly was a whore. To Slocum's surprise, the idea didn't come as anything different than what he had already been thinking deep down.

"So she's new to town." That was a flat statement, and Sparky did not contradict him. "See you later. What time's the evening fun usually begin?"

"Whenever you get here, Slocum." Sparky laughed, pumped his hand and then left. Slocum lingered a moment before stepping into the cold night. The Firehouse No. 7 was suddenly quiet inside, only the lingering stench of burning wood and piss remaining behind to keep the bartender company.

Slocum mounted and turned his horse's face uphill, toward Molly's shack. With housing as scarce as a gambler in church, he wondered how she had found even that ram-shackle place. He rode slowly, making sure he followed the right path. The snow had melted enough to turn the ground into mud trails, each indistinguishable from the next. He soon sighted the right shack. A thin gray wisp of smoke curled from the vent pipe thrust through the roof.

Molly was home.

As he approached, Slocum had the eerie feeling something was wrong. He opened his coat and slid his hand underneath to the cross-draw holster, so his hand rested reassuringly on the ebony handle of his six-shooter. Behind the shack was only one horse, not two. And it was neither of the ones Molly had ridden off with when she left Virginia City in such a hurry.

"What ya want?" A scrawny man stepped from the shack, a sawed-off shotgun in his hand. He held the weapon as if he had little idea how to use it. With a single glance, Slocum sized him up as a prospector. The man might have bought the shotgun to run off claim jumpers but had probably never fired it. That made Slocum even more ill at ease than if he had faced a professional gunslinger. There was no telling what this jumpy prospector would do.

"I'm looking for Molly Preston. She here?"

"Don't know anybody by that name," the prospector said. The man lowered the gun and scratched his head. "Name's familiar, though."

"Molly Preston?"

"Nope, jist the Preston part. Heard of a prospector with that moniker when I was over in Gold Hill, on the other side of this here mountain."

Slocum reckoned the man had just returned from his trip—to his own shack. Molly was a squatter who had moved in when she saw an empty bed. She had acted quick, and the bed hadn't stayed empty long, not with John Slocum to share it with her.

"Might the name be Seamus Preston?"

"That's it. Seamus Preston. Not a likable cuss, not at all. Nasty mean drunk." The prospector lifted the muzzle of the shotgun in Slocum's direction again. "You a partner of his?"

"More like a mailman. Got a package for him. Never met the man."

"Well, he ain't here."

Slocum bided his time. The prospector was a garrulous sort and probably didn't see that many people in any given month.

"He's staked a claim a bit north of here. In Old Glory Canyon."

"The one branching off Liberty Bell?" Slocum asked.

"That's the one. You know this here country purty good." Again the prospector turned suspicious. "You ain't a claim jumper, are you?"

"Just passing through." Slocum politely touched the brim of his hat and rode past, aware that the prospector watched until he found the trail leading in the direction Molly had taken them the first time. But she had diverted them away from the real direction where her brother's mine sank into the hillside. If Seamus Preston even was her brother. Since nothing else about her had proven to be honest, Slocum had to wonder.

He wondered but really didn't care one whit. All he had to do was deliver the map and then return to the Firehouse No. 7 Saloon for a few rounds with his new drinking partners.

It took most of the afternoon to ride deeper into the canyon. As Slocum passed the mouth leading to Liberty Bell Canyon, he saw the mounds of rock he had brought down with the case of old dynamite. The road agents might have escaped. He couldn't tell and didn't want to dig through the debris to find out. More likely, they had been far enough away to avoid the worst of the rockfall. The man he had tied up at the mouth of the mine, however, was a different kettle of fish.

Slocum couldn't work up any sympathy for the man. He should not have tried tracking them down.

He rode steadily through the afternoon up Old Glory Canyon and finally saw a crudely lettered sign: "Preston's Glory Hole." Slocum was not sure this was anything to advertise. Miners working drifts feared the roof caving in on them, opening a hole all the way to the surface—a glory hole. Tons of rock might come crashing down. But he had heard of circumstances where a glory hole exposed an unsuspected vein of ore. Preston might have stumbled on something worthwhile and wouldn't need a torn map sent by his dead brother.

Slocum took the winding trail into the hills, going around a small hillock and then cutting back up a steeper trail. As he rode, he noticed the ground had been cut up, as if a small herd of horses had passed by recently. Then the gunshots echoed down from higher on the slope.

"Damn," Slocum muttered. He reached for his rifle but it was gone. He had lost it when the dynamite had exploded the day before, and he had failed to replace it in Virginia City. Drawing his trusty six-gun, Slocum spurred his tired horse to a quicker gait uphill and around a bend in the road to the side of Preston's mine.

The mine was, indeed, a glory hole. The original opening into the side of the mountain was boarded up. Slocum reckoned Preston had followed a drift around and under the ground in front of the mouth of the mine. The rumble of wagons and heavy equipment had caused the ground to give way, producing what looked like a sinkhole with a ladder poking up out of it.

Downhill stood a shack that might have been the twin of the one where Slocum and Molly had spent the night so pleasurably and that was now occupied once more by its rightful owner. This one had three men poking around outside while another stood guard with his rifle resting in the crook of his left arm.

Slocum didn't bother waiting for them to spot him. He cocked his Colt Navy, took careful aim and squeezed off a shot. He was as lucky as he was good as a marksman. The round caught the rifleman in the gunhand. He screeched like a hoot owl and dropped his rifle. This brought the other three running, guns out.

There were several things Slocum might do. He could turn tail and run. The four men would follow him if he did that. He could stand and fight, but he had probably used up all his luck with that single shot. That left the only sensible course of action.

He attacked.

With a Rebel yell, he put his spurs to his horse's flanks and lowered his head to give the men the smallest possible target. Then he squeezed off shot after shot at the confused, surprised men. The closer he got, the more dangerous it became for Slocum, because he was running low on ammo and dared not swing around and grab the spare Colt Navy from his saddlebags. Instead of breaking off his attack, he changed his tactics.

"Don't let these varmints escape, Sheriff George! Get 'em! Close in on 'em and cut 'em off!" Invoking the lawman's name had a galvanizing effect on the quartet. They broke and ran. This told Slocum all he needed to know. Whatever they were up to, they were afraid of being caught by the law.

By the time Slocum reached the shack, the four owlhoots were gone. He pointed his pistol in the direction they had retreated and pulled the trigger. The hammer fell on an empty chamber.

He had been lucky again.

Slocum swung about, fumbled in his saddlebags and pulled out his spare six-shooter. It saved him the time reloading the one that had ridden in his holster on the trip to the mine.

Slipping from the saddle, Slocum went to the shack

door. It had been kicked in. He peered inside, but the shadows were too dense for him to make out anything.

"Preston? You in there?" When he got no answer, he entered cautiously, the muzzle swinging back and forth to cover anyone laying in wait. The single room was empty. The men who had left in such a hurry had destroyed the simple furnishings, breaking the stool, overturning the table and ripping apart the pallet Preston had used as a mattress. A dynamite crate Preston had used to store the rest of his belongings had been broken apart. Slocum couldn't tell if anything was missing.

What else might the men be looking for but the map? Molly had known about it. The gang that had followed them to the other mine probably knew and had come after him. When Slocum had escaped them, the gang probably thought he had delivered it successfully to Seamus Preston.

Noise from the direction of the mine brought Slocum around. He dashed for the outer corner of the shack and saw a man's head disappearing into the glory hole. The ladder shook as the man hurried down.

"Seamus!" called Slocum. "Your brother sent me. I'm not going to hurt you." He shouted at empty air. Cursing, Slocum stomped to the edge of the pit and peered over, careful not to outline himself against the bright blue afternoon Nevada sky. Getting his head blown off after coming this far wasn't in his battle plan.

From below he heard rustling about, like a rat running through a general store's larder.

"Seamus Preston, come on back here," Slocum called. The words echoed through the drifts below. He saw one side of the drift blocked, the one running back toward the mouth of the mine. The other continued downhill at an angle. Preston had taken that one to escape what he thought was danger.

"I ran the road agents off. Or were they claim jumpers?

They're gone. All I want is to give you a map your brother wanted you to have."

Getting no response, Slocum knew what he had to do. He grasped the rickety ladder and swung around, getting his boots onto the top rung. He had barely started down into the mine when the ladder began to shake. Slocum thought the rungs were coming unnailed. Then he realized the rumbling came from below.

A blast of dust billowed up and shrouded him as surely as any gritty, biting dust storm he had ever endured in West Texas. The drift where Seamus Preston had vanished seconds before collapsed, trapping the prospector in the mine.

8

Slocum clung to the ladder until the dust and heated air had blasted past. He worried that this was from detonation of a gas pocket. If the mineshaft were filled with gas, there would be scant chance for Seamus Preston to escape. A secondary rumble shook Slocum off the ladder. He toppled backward, flailing as he fell. He landed hard on his back and was momentarily stunned.

Choking, he sat up and gasped in huge drafts of air through his bandanna. When the dust finally cleared, he got to shaky feet and looked around. The ladder had tumbled into the pit but was intact. He pushed it upright again and made certain he could get out of the glory hole when he wanted. Slocum realized this was likely to be the way he left Preston's mine, too, since both drifts were closed with rockfall.

He went to the plug in the tunnel Seamus had taken before all hell broke loose. Slocum ran his hands over the broken timbers and saw why the collapse had occurred. The wood was rotted through even at the thickest sections. And Slocum saw that the original timber had been cut razor thin in places. The hills were denuded of trees, telling him that wood was in such demand that corners were cut at every turn. Skimping on timbers supporting the rocky roofs of a mine was suicidal.

Slocum saw the evidence in front of him.

He began digging. The rocks were the size of his head or larger and required considerable effort to move from the blockage to a spot behind him. Before he knew it, he was sweating in the close, tight hole. Slocum never flagged, though. If he didn't reach Seamus Preston quickly enough, the man might die of suffocation.

If he wasn't already dead.

Slocum thought about his next course of action if he found Preston's lifeless body. Turn the map over to Molly? That was the most likely—if he believed she was Seamus Preston's sister, which he didn't. He might try to figure out the map himself, but he had looked at it often enough to know it was a map fragment. Whoever held the rest of it had the compass rose, the legend and information necessary to position the map properly before finding the spot where . . .

What? Where the treasure was buried? Slocum snorted at the idea of wasting time on a map to the Lost Dutchman Mine or whatever it might represent. He dug faster.

Tired, filthy, he succeeded in moving enough rock at the top of the fall to open a space the size of his head. He flopped belly down on the pile and shoved his face forward.

"Are you there?" Slocum shouted. He heard his words echoing down a long tunnel. That heartened him. The drift had not collapsed for any significant length. "Seamus Preston? You all right? My name's Slocum. Your brother sent me." Again, Slocum felt the lack of not even knowing the other Preston's given name.

He listened hard but heard nothing but distant pebbles falling and timbers creaking ominously. Sniffing hard, he tried to detect any gas. A canary was better for such detection, Slocum knew, but he didn't have a bird right now. Another way of finding out if there was firedamp, as the miners called it, was to light a lucifer and then get blown to hell and gone when the gas exploded in his face.

Slocum wanted to try some other approach to finding out if the mine was safe. He kept digging, intending to open the hole enough to let out any pockets of trapped gas that might have accumulated near the blockage.

That was what he intended. He stopped clawing away at the rock when he heard footsteps above him. Looking up, Slocum saw four sets of toes poking over the lip of the hole. He reached for his six-shooter but saw he was in no position to fight.

"Who's down there?" came a voice he almost recognized. "We done heard you scrabblin' about like some kind of mine rat. Who's there?"

A head appeared for a quick peek down.

"Sheriff George," Slocum called up. "It's me, Slocum. I talked to you in town about the road agents out in Liberty Bell Canyon."

"You're a ways from the canyon. This here's Seamus Preston's claim. What're you doin' down there?"

"Trying to get him out. He came down the ladder and vanished into this tunnel, then the roof caved in. I have a small hole dug open, but I can't see him inside."

"You two, go help him," ordered the sheriff. Two deputies with him backed away so their toes vanished from the edge of the hole. Slocum heard heated argument over who would come down to help dig.

Slocum felt the pressure of time weighing him down. Seamus Preston was nowhere in sight, but he might be injured and not far down the drift. Slocum turned back to pulling free the rocks to enlarge the opening so he could wiggle in and explore for himself. He heard the ladder creaking and groaning as someone scampered down.

"Grab a pry bar and give me a hand," Slocum said without looking to see who had come down. "If we get this big rock moved, we could go hunt for him."

"Is Seamus hurt bad?"

Slocum jerked around to face a jet-black-haired woman, her bright blue eyes fixed on him. Her lovely, pale-skinned face was out of place in a world of sunbaked, ugly, leathery ones. She wore a heavy coat that couldn't conceal the curves of her figure.

"You're not a deputy," Slocum said.

"How astute of you," she said with open disdain. "I rode out here with the sheriff and his posse to catch those awful highwaymen."

"The ones from Liberty Bell Canyon?"

She shrugged, then shook her head vigorously. "I have no idea where they might have been. All I am interested in is where they are and how to stop them before they harm Seamus."

"What's he to you?" Slocum asked, not sure he wanted to hear the answer. He had already come across Molly who had claimed to be Preston's sister.

"His sweetheart," the woman answered. "My name's Erin, and I fetched the sheriff to help Seamus. He's been bedeviled by claim jumpers from the first day he staked out this old mine."

"He found a new vein?" Slocum looked at the rock walls and saw nothing that would have made him risk his life in the disused shafts.

"He looks to be rich from pawing around in here," Erin said. "What's this interest in my beau?"

"A long story," Slocum said, not wanting to go into the details, especially where Molly was concerned. At least Erin had not claimed to be Seamus's sister. He turned back to the rockfall and shook his head. "There's no way we can get in there."

"He went into the mine?"

"A few seconds before it collapsed. I tried to spot him, but it's mighty dark in there."

"You were smart enough not to light a match," Erin said. "You've been in mines before?"

"I've been most everywhere," Slocum said.

"How many of them varmints was there, Slocum?" Sheriff George again looked down into the pit. "We got tracks for three of 'em."

"Four, maybe more," Slocum shouted up.

"Don't know if we kin catch 'em," the sheriff said. "Lookin' like a storm brewin' again. Hell of a year for the snow to come this early and it not even harvest moon yet."

"Can you help out, Sheriff?" Slocum pointed to the rocks blocking entry to the mine. The lawman didn't answer directly but sent down two grumbling deputies this time.

Slocum and Erin stood back and let the men cuss and piss and moan over such work. They'd signed up for a posse, one contended, not to move rock. If he had wanted a mining job, he'd have gone to work at the Silver King Mine. As much as the two complained, they worked steadily and weren't tuckered out like Slocum. They had a good-sized hole opened at the top of the fall in less than twenty minutes.

"You boys coming along?" Slocum asked as he stared into the inky depths of the mine. "A man's likely to be in there, injured or maybe dead." He still didn't understand how Seamus Preston had avoided being crushed by the collapsing roof, but there was no evidence that he was under the pile.

"Go in there?" One deputy looked at the other, but both shook their heads. "We're not that dumb."

Slocum did not blame them. If he'd had a choice, he wouldn't have gone into the mine, either. But he was responsible for delivering the map. More than this, he couldn't leave a man who might be seriously injured to die in the dark. Settling his nerves, he scrambled over the crest of the rock pile, down the far side and found himself enveloped in inky darkness. Reaching out to touch the wall to guide himself along, he recoiled when he touched something warm and soft.

"Watch it," Erin said. He had accidentally touched her chest.

"You're coming along when the deputies wouldn't?" Slocum was glad that Erin wasn't squeamish about checking to see if the man was flattened like a swatted mosquito.

"Those deputies are more at home bellied up to a bar, swilling demon rum." Her outrage was directed more at the men's drinking than at their lack of courage. Slocum wondered if Seamus was a teetotaler. His brother certainly had not been, not when he had owned the Stolen Nugget Saloon back in Truckee.

Slocum gingerly reached in the other direction to find the rough wall. He inched along until the opening was far behind, hardly a bright spot the size of a dime. As he crept deeper into the mine, he kept sniffing for gas. The time he had worked in a hard rock mine had been agonizingly backbreaking, and constant danger had ridden in his hip pocket. But he had not been in the dark. A miner's helmet with a carbide lamp had given some light, and miner's candles were always set to cast light on the ore vein he had used his pickax on.

"I might miss him in the dark," Slocum finally said. "I haven't found any drifts branching from this one. Anything on your side?"

Erin said, "Nothing. Just rock. Is it safe to light a match? I know about methane gas, but Seamus never mentioned trouble with it in this drift."

Slocum considered his safest course of action. That was, of course, backtracking and getting the hell out of this potential grave. Since this was out of the question, lighting the lucifers in his pocket seemed better by the minute.

"Hold up," Slocum said. "We can only die once. You sure you want to stay here?"

"You're going to light a match?"

The sudden flare caused Slocum to squint. His first sight as soon as the yellow and blue dots dancing in front of him vanished was Erin. Her dark hair almost merged with the dark rock, but her bright blue eyes and pale face, now streaked with dirt, turned her downright angelic.

"Take a gander around while it's burning," Slocum said. He took his own advice and saw the tunnel stretching far ahead, disappearing into darkness a dozen yards off. He dropped the match when it burned down to his fingers.

"Tracks," Erin said. "I saw tracks."

"Fresh ones," Slocum added. He had seen them, too. It had been years since anyone had been in this deserted section of the mine, and dust had settled from the roof to form a shallow layer on the floor. The dust had been disturbed recently by a single set of boot prints going away from the cave-in. Without a better candidate, Seamus Preston was likely to have left the footprints.

"Did you see anything else? My eyes were dazzled by the flare of the match," Erin said.

"Let's go another twenty paces, and I'll light another lucifer. I'll warn you so you can look away." Slocum advanced slowly, worried that he might not have seen a pit in the floor. If the mine could collapse all the way to the surface, the lower drifts might fall into still lower ones.

"Did Seamus explore all these shafts or was he working somewhere else?" Slocum asked.

"What difference does it make?"

"You're about the most suspicious filly I've come across in quite a spell," Slocum said. "I want to get him out of here in one piece. Anything that might help him is worth knowing."

"Sorry," Erin said. "I'm not acquainted with you. I don't know why you were even looking for Seamus."

"Business. His brother sent me with a letter for him."

"Him?" Erin snorted in disgust. "All Michael ever did was get Seamus into trouble."

Slocum had learned a bit more. Preston's name was Michael. Or was Erin testing him?

"How many brothers and sisters does Seamus have?" He stopped, tapped ahead a few inches and found the drift angling to the left. Slocum tried to estimate how far they had come and couldn't. Considering their pace, they might be under the hillside on the far slope of the canyon. Slocum knew mining companies ran with the veins of ore, going wherever the "color" took them and devil take the hindmost. Some claims were crisscrossed with holes that would collapse, one by one, over the years and make traveling aboveground a nightmare.

"Do you hear that?" Erin reached out and touched his arm. Her fingers clenched down hard. "It sounds like a man struggling to take a breath."

"Close your eyes. I'm lighting another match." Slocum pulled the lucifer from the small tin box and struck it against the rock wall. He took his own advice and kept his eyes tightly shut until the flare died. Holding the match high above his head, he saw how the flame and smoke from the fiery tip flattened out into a right angle to the matchstick.

"Look quick at the floor," Slocum said as he craned his neck upward. The match flame sucked up toward a chimney in the roof. Slocum wasn't sure but thought he saw a bright star or two—a sure sign the rock chimney opened onto the mountain across the valley from the entrance.

Slocum let the match burn his fingers before dropping it. "What did you see?"

"The tracks . . ." Erin sounded unsure of herself. "They just ended. I don't understand."

"He climbed up a rock vent to get out. It looks natural but was widened to provide air in the mine." Slocum knew such vents were also dangerous. Any gas explosion would race through the tunnels and surge upward to turn the mine into a blast furnace that would burn far longer than it ought to.

"Are you sure he went that way?"

"You didn't see tracks going on." Slocum struck another match and examined the chimney walls for scratches. He saw scuff marks all the way to the top.

"I can make it," Erin said, seeing the expression on his face. "Go on, go first and I'll follow."

"You first," Slocum said, coming to a swift decision. "I'm bulkier than you."

"You want to catch me if I fall?" She seemed amused at the notion. "Very well." Erin spit on her hands, let Slocum give her a boost and worked her way upward in the dark. Slocum caught occasional glimpses of an arm or leg or other delightful portions of her anatomy as she scaled the rock fissure. Then she disappeared.

"Are you all right?" Slocum called.

"I'm on the side of the mountain. The far side, I think. There's snow all around, and tracks lead away."

Slocum grumbled as he started his own journey up the tight-walled crevice. His shoulders were rubbed raw by the time he popped out onto the ground. If he had been riding past on the mountain, he might not have seen this opening, but that hardly mattered. Once again he was out of the rocky grave below and under the open sky.

"Looks like it'll snow soon," Erin said. "The sheriff was right."

Slocum heard the hesitancy in her voice. She wanted to catch up with her sweetheart but also wanted to return to the safety of Sheriff George's posse on the other side of the mountain.

"Why'd he hightail it like that?" Slocum knelt and caught starlight reflected off the snowpack, showing Seamus's long stride. He had not just left; he had left in a mighty big hurry.

"What would you do if you'd just been beset by thieves wanting to kill you and steal your claim?"

"I wouldn't have headed in the opposite direction after getting out of the mine," Slocum said. "If he didn't know the terrain well, I'd say he was mixed up about direction." He looked at Erin and saw the answer. Seamus Preston had explored every square inch of this valley and knew it well. Although he might not have wanted to fight off the owl-hoots after his claim, why hadn't he wanted to spy on them from the top of the mountain? He could have waited until they had left and then salvaged what he could from his cabin.

"He didn't know I was coming with the sheriff and his posse, if you can call those craven types that."

"Why'd you fetch the sheriff?"

"We'd been harassed by those ruffians for days. I refused to allow it to go on, but Seamus has a head as hard as any of that rock. He could handle it himself, he said."

The stars blinked out as thin tendrils of cloud blew past. Then those wisps of clouds turned into something more substantial. Slocum turned up his coat collar as a polar wind whipped across the stony face of the mountain.

"We've got to get back to your camp," he said. "There's a storm threatening."

"All the more reason to find Seamus. He's frightened and on the run and doesn't have any supplies."

"We don't, either," Slocum pointed out.

"You do as you please, sir. I'll find him. How hard can it be? He left a trail a blind man could follow."

Slocum saw how it disappeared into the night. He found himself tossed on the horns of a dilemma. If Seamus had taken cover in a nearby stand of oak and maple, finding him would be quick. They could be in his shack boiling coffee and arguing over what few provisions Slocum carried in his saddlebags. But if the prospector had kept going at the clip he had as he left the rock chimney, they might never catch up. Slocum had to follow the trail. All Seamus had to do was blaze it.

"You head to the mountain crest and go back to the shack. Wait for us there. If the sheriff's men are still around, send them with my horse."

"I am not your errand girl," Erin said tartly. "He's my man. I won't turn my back on him when he needs me most."

"Then step lively," Slocum said. "We've got a lot of distance to make up between him and us."

The snowflakes began fluttering down before they reached the edge of the forest. By the time they had followed Seamus Preston's tracks to the far side of the trees, the wind had picked up and blew the snow against their faces in a blinding fury.

9

"We ought to go back to the mine," Erin said, shivering. She hugged herself, but her coat wasn't up to the task of holding in body heat against the teeth of a north wind. The dark-haired woman repeatedly wiped snow from her face, until it became obvious she could never keep up. The snow was reaching blizzard proportions.

"Which way is it?" Slocum asked. He had come to the same conclusion some time earlier and had tried to figure out which way to go. He had guided them back upslope in an attempt to reach the mountain's crest, but the snow was beginning to drift, making it harder to guess which way led to safety.

"I thought you knew."

Slocum had to shout against the howl of the wind.

"No idea. We've got to find shelter quick or we'll freeze." He and Molly had ridden out one storm. Delightfully so, before he had begun to mistrust her.

"I see something dark ahead," Erin said. "It—" She tripped and fell headlong into the gathering snow. For a moment, she struggled to come up to her knees and made strange patterns in the new snow with both arms and legs. Then she hesitated a moment, reached down and ran her

87

hand over the cause of her fall. She pushed away and let out a loud scream of pure anguish.

"What's wrong?" Then Slocum saw what the woman had stumbled over. He knelt and brushed away the half inch of snow that had blown over Seamus Preston's lifeless body. He rolled the man onto his back and felt a cold lump that had nothing to do with the weather form in the pit of his stomach.

Seamus had been stabbed repeatedly in the belly and chest, leaving his chest and the ground under his body a bloody morass. Whoever had been after him had found him.

"He's dead," Erin said in a tiny voice that was almost drowned out by the rising wind. "What are we going to do?"

"Get to shelter, if we can," Slocum said. "He's not going to be eaten by wolves in this storm, and he won't start rotting until he thaws."

"Oh." Erin gulped and looked even paler than usual. She got to her feet, tottered and almost fell.

"Sorry," Slocum said, knowing the sight of the woman's murdered lover affected her more than it ever could him. He had seen too many bodies in his day to be overly upset finding a man he did not even know. All Seamus's death meant to him was being unable to deliver the map. The most tragic part was Seamus dying not knowing his brother was also dead.

"Bury him," Erin said. "I'll bury him. It's the proper thing to do since he's dead." The woman's face was locked into a mask of grief. Slocum knew the signs of shock when he saw them. He didn't want to add frostbite to them.

"It'll wait," Slocum said. "Let the storm blow through."

"I killed him. I mean, I was responsible." She clutched her throat and wobbled a tad more. Slocum got his arm around her in time to keep her from fainting dead away. Over her feeble protests, he steered her away from Seamus's body. His appraisal of the situation hadn't changed. The only thing that would happen to the man's corpse was that it might freeze through and through. Otherwise, it was safe from predators of all stripes.

"A mine shaft," Slocum said, looking at the cinderlike tailings crunching underfoot. Not even the blowing snow could hide the ugly black residue. He followed the black stream like it was a road to the mouth of a boarded-up mine. All the ore must have petered out in this vicinity for so many of the mines to be shuttered.

Gripping the boards, Slocum pulled a few free and then stacked them just inside. Why anybody had bothered to board up the shaft was beyond him. This was a waste of valuable lumber. As he pushed Erin ahead of him to keep her from returning to Seamus's body, he saw why the place had been boarded up. Someone had stored a considerable amount of supplies here and had wanted to keep them out of sight.

"We hit the mother lode," he told her. "Cases of canned fruit and even some bacon all done up in salt." He also saw crates with U.S. Army stamped on the side. Someone had stolen enough rifles from the Army to start a small war. Alongside was a mound of ammo. "Why don't you get to fixing us some food?"

Slocum looked around to see Erin stumbling toward the mouth of the mine, intent on returning to Seamus Preston's side. He grabbed her, swung her around and forced her to sit on a crate.

"Stay here. If you go out in that storm, you're going to die."

"They killed him because of me. He thought I could keep it safe, but when they didn't find it, they killed him." Again her hand went to her throat. Then she burst into tears.

"I'll fix the food," Slocum said. He built a fire pit just inside the mine and used some of the lumber to start a fire. He decided there was no reason to skimp and added enough to make a roaring bonfire. The smoke was sucked out of the cave by the wind, and the heat radiated back, making it warm enough for him to strip off his heavy coat. In the pile of stolen goods, he found a dozen or more Army blankets and spread these on the floor a ways back from the fire. Then he set about fixing supper.

"Here," he said, handing Erin an empty tin can to use as a crude bowl. "Eat. You need to keep up your strength."

"I never thought they'd find him like that. He was always so . . . so alert. Seamus slept with his hand on his six-gun. I didn't like it, but now I understand why he did it. He knew they would kill him."

"Who're you talking about?"

"I don't know their names. They were partners. Michael got him involved in something so terribly wrong that he would never tell me about it. He was ashamed of what he'd done. But Michael was proud of it. I think it was a robbery that turned bloody. I don't know."

Slocum rested his hand on the map in his pocket. This might be an actual treasure map he was supposed to deliver to Seamus Preston. A real prize and not some fictitious hoard born of long hours of solitude as a prospector slowly went crazy. Slocum had to decide what to do with the map. The lure of gold from such a robbery was a powerful one for him. If it had already been stolen, why return it? He could claim it as salvage, like seafaring captains did when they came upon a wreck.

"Did Seamus and Michael have any brothers or sisters?" he asked.

"Why are you so keen on that?" Erin asked. "Seamus never mentioned anyone other than Michael. He was mighty closemouthed when it came to his family. I don't think either of them had a decent mother, and all he ever said of his pa was how the man spent every possible minute of the day drunk as an English lord."

"Which is why Seamus was a teetotaler?"

"How'd you know?" Erin looked at him with new admiration. "I must be careful around you. You listen to what a body says."

Slocum was a mite hesitant to say what Erin's body was telling him now. She had loosened her coat and sat closer to the blazing fire. The woman's normally pale face was flushed now, though Slocum might have imagined that, as the rosy glare from the fire added highlights to her fair skin. It might even have been some frostbite from their exposure out in the wind. Or it might have been more.

"John," she said in a small voice. "My world's been turned upside down today. I've lost the man I loved most, almost died myself, and now I can't think of anything but how the men who killed Seamus will come after me."

"Why's that?" he asked. "What were they looking for?"

"Seamus trusted me with his secret. I'm not sure I should put your life at risk by telling you."

She peeled off her coat and set it neatly, patting it into a pillow on the stack of blankets he had laid out for her.

"That's up to you," Slocum said, but he could guess what it might be. If Michael Preston had sent half a map to his brother, that meant Seamus had the other part. Placed together, the map might lead a man so inclined to where loot from a big robbery had been hidden. Molly had certainly known of the map, and Erin was hinting that she had the other part.

Slocum wasn't sure what to do. Molly had been underhanded and an obvious liar but could he be sure Erin was any better? All he had to go on was that she and Sheriff George had shown up with a few deputized men in a posse. Slocum had never found pinning a badge on a man's chest to make him any more honest. Sometimes, it was just the reverse. A good man turned rotten with power.

If there was enough gold at stake, Sheriff George might throw in with Erin to grab a cut. For all that, Slocum had nothing but the woman's word that she and Seamus had even been lovers. There had been no trace of a woman's presence in the shack, but it had been well searched and mostly destroyed.

"Everything I do is up to me," Erin said, her blue eyes bold. "It's true, you know. I hadn't believed it, but Michael claimed it was so."

"What's true?" Slocum watched in fascination as Erin kept stripping off layer after layer of clothing. He looked away once and saw snowflakes fluttering through the fire, turning into instant raindrops that became steam. But beyond, the dancing flakes took on the eerie aspect of red fireflies. He turned back from the swirl of snow to see that Erin was bare to the waist. In spite of the heat from the fire, she shivered a little and gooseflesh covered her sleek alabaster skin. Her nipples hardened into ruddy cherries surrounded by bumpy, coppery rings atop mounds whiter than the snow.

Raven's-wing-dark hair, bright blue eyes, skin clear and white and breasts firm like twin apples—Slocum felt himself responding.

"What's true is that Michael said that a brush with death makes a body feel . . . horny. I had thought it was more of his blarney, but it's not, is it?" Erin lay back on the blanket, lifted her buttocks off the blanket and began wiggling out of her skirts. When she was completely naked and stretched out on the blanket, she stared at him in bold challenge. "Do you feel that way? That death makes you want to reaffirm life?"

"Never thought on it," Slocum said. He was getting powerful uncomfortable in his jeans. "Might be the death has to be personal."

"You've seen so much, haven't you, John?"

"The war—and after," he said, unwilling to dwell on the oceans of blood and bodies that he had seen stacked like cordwood. He had been responsible for some of the blood and not a few of those bodies, but seldom had anyone died who meant that much to him. Slocum had learned that caring meant nothing but pain.

"Help me ease my pain," Erin said, as if reading his mind. "We both need to ease our ache—the ache of a tormented soul." She tossed her head and got a pendant moved around behind her out of the way, so only a gold chain circled her perfect neck.

Slocum kicked free of his boots and dropped his gunbelt before getting out of his jeans. He kept his eyes fixed on the lovely woman stretched so enticingly for him. From head to foot and back he studied every luscious curve of her recumbent body. He had thought her breasts were her finest quality, but that had been after she had stripped down for him. Before, he had thought her portrait-perfect face had been the most beguiling he had seen in a month of Sundays. But now he was unsure. Her legs were sculpted by an artist, and the dark furry triangle hidden between her legs was as powerful as any magnet he had ever felt. He was drawn to her inexorably.

Slocum dropped down but was in too much of a rush to let Erin peel back his shirt to get him as naked as she was. Bending low, he kissed her hand, worked up her arm and then lavished full attention to her ear and cheek and luscious lips. She responded with gusto. Her arms went around his neck and pulled him down fully against her trembling body. He felt her lust-hard nipples poking into his chest, and this spurred him on. If there had been any question as to her intentions before, it was gone now.

Whatever her reasons for wanting him, he wanted her as fervently.

He broke off the kiss and worked his way down her body, to the deep chasm between her breasts. Switching from one tip to the other, he alternately kissed and suckled like a newborn babe until she was thrashing about under him with desires running wild.

Of their own accord, her sleek, slender legs parted and revealed the trembling nether lips that had been partially hidden to him before. Slocum worked his way down her belly to the spot and then thrust out his tongue. Erin went wild with need. Her legs parted even more as she lifted off the pile of blankets to get more of his oral loving.

"Yes, oh, I'm on fire inside. Don't stop, John. Never stop. Oh, oh!"

He gave her a tongue-lashing that drove her crazy with need. Then he left the tasty morsel and worked down the insides of her legs, kissing, licking, lightly nipping. She became incoherent by the time he had gone down one leg and all the way back up the other. He rubbed his stubbled chin against her tender flesh and got a response so intense it left him blind and suffocating for a moment as she clamped her legs around his head.

The tender rictus passed and Erin sank back to the blankets. Sweat beaded her fine skin, and she looked a bit dazed.

"Never felt like that before," she mumbled. She half sat up and looked at him, but something had caught his attention that he had missed before. The pendant on the gold chain she had swung behind her now had fallen between her ample breasts. Firelight glinted off a twin to the sawed-in-half gold coin he had taken from the dead outlaw.

Erin didn't have the other half of the map. She wore the gold coin that completed the one he had hidden away beneath his shirt. All this passed through Slocum's mind in a flash.

"Don't stop, John. I couldn't stand it. I feel like a raw nerve. I'm tingling all over. I . . . I need more."

"So do I," he said. He stroked gently along the woman's outer thighs, then reared back, gripped down hard on her posterior and twisted, rolling her onto her belly.

"What do you want me to do, John?"

"Up on your hands and knees."

Erin obeyed with an eagerness that matched Slocum's own need. He moved in behind her, scooting forward on his knees until the curve of his groin pressed fully against her silky, rounded buttocks. He felt her trembling like a horse eager for a race. Then he entered her from behind, his manhood slipping easily into her moist, tight female passage.

"Oh, oh," she gasped out. "So big. You're so big, John. Ride me hard, ride me like you're breaking a bronco!"

He reached around her waist and braced himself, then thrust fully into her. Every last inch of his steely length slipped into her sheath, then withdrew as quickly. He caught sight of the half coin swinging back and forth under her, occasionally catching firelight. Gold, pure gold, and a clue to finding more gold. But he knew he had struck a different kind of pay dirt as he slid forward and vanished within her tender, clutching, clinging body. She enveloped him totally, then began squeezing down around him.

Slocum grunted and withdrew, only to race back. It was cold outside; it was burning hot within. He wanted more. Hips swinging in an ages old rhythm, he built the carnal pressures within both of their bodies. Erin began ramming her hips back to meet his inward thrust, and added to the tensions mounting in their loins.

Slocum felt the bubbling cauldron deep within threaten to explode. He slowed, but the woman was too insistent with the motions of her hips, her body, those parts within that so excited him. Slocum could not rest, so he returned to his thrusting with renewed vigor, until he passed the point of no return.

He grabbed Erin's hips with both hands as she shuddered and tried to fall forward onto the blankets. That wouldn't do. He was close and couldn't slip free until he was finished. But sexual release having riven her, the woman's muscles turned to jelly and she sank forward to lie facedown. Slocum followed her forward, never withdrawing, and discovered even greater sensation ripping through him. Her fleshy rump pressed sensually into him as he drove downward. She elevated herself just enough to give a new angle of entry that rubbed and stroked along the most sensitive portion of Slocum's anatomy. She realized what effect she had on him and did all she could to give him pleasure equal to that which she had already experienced. Erin twitched and turned and excited him until he could no longer control himself.

He spilled his seed, then continued his powerful strokes until he melted like an icicle in the morning sun. Slocum sank full length on top of the woman, then rolled to one side as she drew up to face him.

Side by side, faces bare inches apart, they lay gazing at one another. Slocum had no idea what went through the woman's mind, but he couldn't help staring at the gold pendant around her neck, so enticingly resting on her firm, full breast.

A double treat.

Erin snuggled closer and put her head onto his shoulder. Then she drifted off to sleep after Slocum pulled the blankets up over them. It took him a while longer to fall asleep, visions of feminine beauty and gold refusing to leave him be.

10

Slocum awoke before Erin and looked at the woman. He reached out and lightly touched the half gold double eagle coin on the chain around her neck. She stirred, murmured something and then rolled onto her back, giving Slocum a view not only of the coin but the woman's breasts. He wanted to dig out the coin he had taken off the outlaw and compare it with the woman's, but he knew she would wake up if he tried. He looked as closely as he could at the coin, but Erin's eyes still popped open.

"What are you doing?" she asked.

Slocum covered his interest in the coin the best way he could think of. He bent over and lightly kissed each of her breasts.

"Good morning," he said.

"That certainly makes it a better morning," Erin said. She stretched like a cat in the sun, then settled down. Slocum saw the slow change in her expression. She had started out happy, but the memory of finding Seamus Preston and the reasons for his death erased her mood.

"We can bury him," Slocum suggested. The snow had stopped during the night, leaving a bright, shiny new day with skies rivaling Erin's eyes and even a warmth out of place after a storm had dumped two inches of snow on the ground.

"Why not?" Erin sat up and shivered. She pulled a blanket around her shoulders. Slocum had the feeling of the final curtain closing on the stage, signaling the exit of the actors and the end of the play.

"The ground'll be frozen, but maybe not too deep. Digging in rocky country like this will be a bigger problem."

"Too bad we can't send him home to Ireland. He was from County Kerry, you know."

Slocum didn't. He knew nothing about the family he had become enmeshed with. Erin went on about the Emerald Isle and how she had followed Seamus when he came to America, but Slocum's thoughts drifted from the tale of woe and young love. He had half the map and half of a mysterious coin. Both were clues to the location of what might be a robber baron's treasure trove. Too many men were willing to kill to get the map for the reward to be a few dollars. Slocum had seen eight men back at Liberty Bell Canyon when he and Molly had escaped.

The thought of Molly churned. Was she Preston's sister? Erin had not exactly denied it. She had only said Seamus Preston had said nothing about having a sister, but Molly had been mighty skittish when it came to facing Sheriff George and had been like a cuckoo sneaking into another bird's nest when she used the miner's shack while he was gone. Simply move in, call it her own, seduce Slocum and then try to steal the map.

As Erin went about getting into her clothes, Slocum saw the coin swaying delightfully. Then she buttoned her blouse and hid both her feminine charms and the coin. The dark-haired beauty saw him watching her and smiled weakly.

"You are a good man, John. But—"

"Not your type?" he finished for her.

"I didn't mean it that way," she said. "We met under . . .

odd circumstances. Seamus dying, the claim jumpers, the storm, last night." A tiny smile crept to the corners of her mouth. It vanished as quickly as it was born. "May I be frank?"

Slocum nodded.

"I don't know if I can trust you at all. Why were you at Seamus's claim? How did the cave-in happen?"

"I didn't cause it."

"Probably not. Seamus had warned me about going into the mine because of the rotted timbers. He feared that his digging would bring down the roof eventually, and it might have."

"I was with Seamus's brother when he died. He wanted me to give Seamus a legacy."

"A legacy," snorted Erin. She began poking through the stack of crates to find something for breakfast. There was no dearth of canned goods to pick from. "The man was a liar, a braggart and not to be trusted."

"He got Seamus involved in the robbery?"

She looked at him sharply. "I may have said more to you than I intended."

"I have half a map I was to give to Seamus," Slocum said. "It might show where the loot was hidden."

Erin heaved a soulful sigh, sat on a crate and put her face in her hands. She began sobbing.

"I told him to have nothing to do with that worthless brother of his, but he wouldn't listen." She looked up. Her blue eyes brimmed with tears. "He has this weighing down his soul now that he is dead and gone. I can only hope St. Peter understands and lets him through the Pearly Gates rather than damning him for all eternity."

"What happened?"

"I don't know the details, but Seamus, Michael and a dozen others hijacked a gold shipment in the middle of Geiger Pass. It was going to San Francisco and the greedy bankers there. They had extorted the gold from the mine owners. Phony use permits, rights of way—those banker fellows did not miss a single thing to charge for. Some contracts were for guaranteed future shipments. Oh, they collected a great, grand wagon train of gold."

"Wagon train?" Slocum perked up. He had been thinking in terms of a strongbox filled with gold dust. This was truly a prize worth seeking if Erin wasn't exaggerating.

"Ten wagonloads. So much they could not make off with it all in a hurry, so they hid it."

"Why'd they need a map?"

"Do you think a banker will allow even a penny to be stolen from him? The robbers were tracked down and killed, some of them. But three families were involved and as one robber died, he passed along a segment of the map to someone else in his family. Someone who had not taken part in the robbery."

"But Seamus and his brother had taken part, so they knew where the gold was stashed. Why didn't they go fetch it for themselves?"

"Seamus stole horses for the gang but wasn't actually there when the gold was stolen or hidden. Michael assured him of an equal share because he was there."

With the bankers so intent on killing the men responsible for the robbery, it made sense to let the bulk of the loot remain hidden until the heat died down. Unfortunately, it looked as if the Pinkertons or whatever detectives the bankers had set on the trail had killed off a goodly number of the participants. The families of the surviving robbers were intent on eliminating their partners and looked to have been successful with the Preston brothers. That reduced the contenders for the gold to two families of road agents.

"I don't want any part of such tainted gold," Erin said.

Slocum pulled the map from his pocket and held it up. She stared at it, then broke into tears again.

"That sheet of paper killed Michael and Seamus. I want nothing to do with it. I only want what's mine, by right."

"What's that?" Slocum asked. He tucked the map back into his pocket.

"The claim. I want Seamus's claim. It was something he worked for, hard, and he got enough gold from the mine to make a living."

"Scavenging petered-out mines is hardly a living," Slocum said.

"It's an honest living. It's not like taking gold drenched in blood."

Slocum didn't bother telling her that gold washed clean mighty easy, but his situation was still unusual. He had promised to deliver the map to Seamus and now couldn't, unless he wanted to throw it into the man's grave before covering him up. He ought to give it to Molly, if she was actually Seamus's sister.

"I'll go back to Virginia City and register my claim. Nobody will contest it. Everyone thinks the mine has been picked clean."

"You intending to work it yourself?"

"If I have to, for a while. I don't know. But it's mine by right. Seamus owes me that much." Erin sniffed, wiped her eyes and went back to fixing breakfast for them. Slocum poked around and found rusty tools. Without a word, he left and went to locate the body of the man causing so much trouble.

It took almost an hour to dig a grave deep enough, but Slocum finished, wrapped the body in a blanket from the cave and rolled Seamus Preston's remains into the hole. By the time he had replaced the dirt, Erin came, holding a small cross she had made. Slocum let her say a few words, then they both went back to the cave in silence.

Erin had eaten before going to the grave. Somehow, Slocum could not find an appetite.

●   ●   ●

The hike back to Seamus Preston's cabin took longer than
Slocum anticipated. Snow blanketed the mountainside and
turned the path slippery. By midday, the frozen slush had
turned to slick mud. A little after noon they reached the
vent from the mineshaft. For an instant only, Slocum considered sliding back down that chimney to the tunnel and
retracing their steps. The idea of being trapped under so
many tons of rock barely supported by rotting timbers kept
him moving to the crest of the mountain.

From there the cabin lay only two miles off. It was twilight when they found the dubious shelter of the ram-
shackle building.

"We'd better stay here for the night," Slocum said.
"Looks like the sheriff took our horses with him when he
left."

"Where'd he get off to?" wondered Erin. "Why not
leave our horses?"

"He didn't know if we would return anytime soon,"
Slocum said. He did not add, *or if we would ever return*.
They would be lucky if Sheriff George didn't sell their
horses back in Virginia City for what he could get.

"It's a long walk into Virginia City," said Erin.

"You can stay here and I'll fetch the horses," Slocum
said. It had been strained between them all the way from
Seamus Preston's grave. He thought Erin was feeling
guilty for having slept with him when Seamus wasn't even
in his grave.

"I have to see to transferring the deed into my name."
Erin sat on the cot and pursed her lips. "It might cost me a
few dollars, but it will be worth every penny. With luck, I
can find enough gold in the drifts to prove Seamus was
right."

"Prove him right about what?"

"Why, everyone said this was a good-for-nothing claim.
I aim to prove them all wrong. And make a few dollars to

live on while doing it." Erin sat primly, hands folded in her lap. She spoke more to convince herself than Slocum about the rightness of her course. Slocum didn't want to disturb her with picayune questions like why the land office would give her the deed since she was not married to Seamus.

Erin hadn't been married, but Molly might be his sister. If true, Molly inherited the mine. That would set Erin off. It also raised the question gnawing away at Slocum like a wolf with a deer haunch. What did he owe Michael Preston and his memory now that his brother was dead?

"I looked around. The sheriff is likely to swing back this way before going to Virginia City," he said. "He won't leave us in the lurch."

"I don't trust him. Seamus didn't. No reason I should, either, although he is the only lawman within fifty miles."

"Seamus didn't trust him because the sheriff would have arrested him if he had known about his part in the robbery."

"Stop it, John. Stop it now! I don't want to hear any more about that awful robbery." Erin clapped her hands to her ears and turned away. Her shoulders shook but she didn't start crying again.

Slocum knew better than to say a word. He slipped out of the cabin and went to the hole. He had meant what he had said about the sheriff and his posse returning. Slocum doubted they would be successful catching the owlhoots who had hurrahed Seamus and tried to get the map from him.

Reaching into his pocket, Slocum pulled out the map and stared at it. A wild thought flashed through his mind. Could this formerly abandoned mine be where the road agents had stashed their ten wagonloads of gold? That would explain Seamus's insistence on remaining at a played-out mine. He wasn't the lily-white saint Erin thought him to be. He might even have played a larger role in the robbery than stealing horses for the gang's getaway.

Slocum turned the map fragment around and around,

fitting it to the terrain. It matched exactly and meant nothing. He realized how the map could indicate just about any valley he had seen in the Sierras. There had to be more.

He pulled out the half coin from under his shirt and turned it over in his fingers. It was the mirror half of the one dangling about Erin's swanlike neck. The completed coin along with the map half might be enough to find the gold. He heard footsteps behind him and hastily tucked away both map and coin.

"I wanted to apologize, John. Seamus shouldn't have died like he did, and it spooked me."

"You've been under a considerable strain," Slocum allowed. Erin stood beside him, staring down into the dark pit. The sun had finally dipped behind the mountain to the west, casting long shadows across the canyon.

"That's no excuse." She reached up to play with the coin pendant.

Slocum commented on it. She smiled almost shyly and drew it out from under her blouse to look at it.

"Seamus gave it to me. He said our love was as pure as gold."

"There's only half a coin."

"Two hearts beating as one."

"He had the matching half?" This surprised Slocum. Did the coin mean anything at all if Seamus had one, also?

"I . . . I don't know. I never thought to ask. I suppose he did."

Before Slocum could ask to examine the coin more closely, the rhythmic *clop-clop-clop* of approaching horses brought him around.

"You were right about almost everything. Forgive me for not believing you," Erin said.

Sheriff George and three of his deputies rode into the camp. Slocum's and Erin's horses trailed behind, looking bored and tired at the same time.

"Good to see you folks're still in one piece. More'n I

can say 'bout one of my posse. The damn outlaws got old Lead Bottom."

"Shot him clean outta the saddle," piped up a deputy. "We had to bury Lead Bottom Freddy where he fell."

"Shut up, Lucas," the sheriff said. "These good people don't care none about that." He cleared his throat and continued. "Did you find Preston?"

"Somebody found him before us," Slocum said. "They stabbed him to death and let him bleed all over the rocks."

"A shame. I liked Seamus. Well, I liked him a little," Sheriff George said, choosing to tell the truth rather than sugarcoat it. "Looks like we drew a bum hand this time. The outlaws got clean away and Seamus got himself killed."

"We found something mighty strange, Sheriff," Slocum went on. He told George about the cave filled with supplies and how it had been boarded over to keep anyone from poking about, should they spot something inside.

"Now why would anybody go and cache food and guns like that?" Sheriff George rubbed his chin and looked from Erin to Slocum and back. "You know any miners in these hills who'd do that, ma'am?"

"No, no one, Sheriff," Erin said. "We never saw many miners or prospectors. The mountains around here are played out."

"But you and Seamus, you two stayed. That's mighty queer, if you ask me."

"Then it's a good thing no one asked you, Sheriff," Slocum said sharply. "What the lady is asking you for, though, is some help."

"Done what I could to catch them rascals," George said.

"She needs to transfer the deed to this property from Seamus's name to hers."

"Now we can't go and do that," the lawman said. "Women can't own real property. That's the law."

"Then can Mr. Slocum get the deed put into his name?"

Erin looked expectantly at Slocum. He cursed himself for getting mixed up in this.

"So you can stay on, but on *his* property?" The sheriff nodded slowly. "If there's no complaints from anybody in town, don't see why not. But you staying on, well now, that would be up to whatever rent Slocum would charge you, wouldn't it?"

Slocum held his temper. He wanted to punch the arrogant son of a bitch for the smirk and the innuendo.

"Let's get to the land office and see to the details," Slocum said, grabbing the reins to his horse. He and Erin rode back to Virginia City side by side, and again they found precious little to say to one another.

11

"Ain't no way I kin do a thing like that," the clerk in the land office said. "We got rules. And that goes 'gainst jist 'bout all the rules in this here book." He put his hand on a thick volume on the end of the counter. From the amount of dust on it Slocum guessed it didn't get as much use as the clerk made out.

"The man's dead. I buried him with my own two hands." Slocum put his hands on the counter and slowly tightened them into fists until the knuckles turned white. The clerk took a half step back and licked his lips.

"Don't get riled up, mister. I got the law on my side. You cain't threaten me none. Bigger men'n you try all the time."

"Reach for that shotgun under the counter, and it'll be the last thing you do on this green Earth."

"How'd you know I—" The clerk spun and stared. Slocum had seen the shotgun in a mirror on the clerk's desk that he had been using to shave himself when Slocum had entered the office.

"There's no need for anyone to get hurt," Slocum said, trying to sound reasonable. He was reaching the end of his rope. He wanted to settle the matter of Seamus Preston's mine, transferring title to Erin, before he moved on. He snorted a little as that thought flitted through his head. As much as he liked the notion of leaving behind Virginia City, the gang trying to find the map and everything else in the boomtown, he knew he was going to stay.

Why waste all that fine booty on a pack of howling wolves? He could be mighty rich for a long, long time if he dipped into that golden pond just a little.

"Glad you see it my way. I got to be sure the next o' kin gets the property. You ain't claimin' yer it, are you?"

"There isn't a next of kin, other than—" Slocum cut off his notion of naming Molly.

"How's that?"

"Nobody's come by saying they were related to Preston, have they?" Slocum asked.

"Nope. And I cain't transfer title to the land to this here woman, Erin Finnigan did you say?"

"What happens to the claim if it doesn't go to Preston's next of kin?"

"County seizes it for taxes, then sells it. Piece of fine property like that'd go for, say, five hunnerd dollars."

Slocum left the land office without another word. Such a princely sum was out of the question since Seamus had bought it for less than twenty dollars, but even that much was beyond Erin's resources. If she didn't get it for only a small transfer fee, she would have to abandon the property. Slocum didn't count that as a bad thing. It was ridiculous to have such a fine-looking woman scrabbling through mountains of filthy tailings and clawing at worthless rock in a dangerous mine for a few specks of gold.

Erin waited for him outside. Slocum hardly had the heart to tell her he couldn't even get the title transferred into his name to give to her. She read his expression perfectly, saving him the trouble of thinking up the right words.

"It's not mine, is it? They wouldn't give it to me, no

matter that I shared bed and work with him." Erin looked disconsolate. "What am I going to do?"

"There's another way. I met a woman who said she was Seamus's sister. If a transfer can be made to me in her behalf, she'd sell out for a song and a dance." Slocum didn't add that Molly would probably sell the mine for stage fare to Carson City. She didn't have any more money than Erin.

"She would never do that," Erin said, frowning. "She'd want a lot of money just because someone else wanted the property. That's the way everyone is in these parts."

"I can add a bit to sweeten the pot," Slocum said. He involuntarily touched his pocket where he kept the map. Swapping a worthless piece of paper for a worthless mine might be the only way everyone ended up happy.

Everyone except John Slocum. He wanted some of the loot stolen in the robbery, if it was as grand a sum as Erin said. Ten wagonloads of gold was a powerful incentive for him to make certain Molly and Erin were willing to cut him in as a partner. Molly obviously knew of the map and Erin wished she didn't.

"I don't know how to repay you, John. You don't have to do any of this. From what you say, you didn't even know Michael very well, much less Seamus."

"I'll think of something," he said. Erin recoiled and looked at him with wide eyes.

"You don't mean . . ." Erin was shocked as her imagination ran wild.

"The pendant around your neck. The one Seamus gave you. It's mighty attractive. That would be a decent payment if I can get you the title free and clear."

"It's all Seamus ever gave me, except woe," she said. Then she looked up into his green eyes and came to a decision. "I'll never forget his love. What's a gold coin mean?"

Slocum almost asked her for it now but refrained.

"I need to find Molly. I'm not sure she's really Seamus and Michael's sister, but if she can pass herself off good enough to convince the land office clerk, I'm not going to argue."

"It seems so dishonest."

"You worry too much. Think of this as a way of cutting corners. That's your claim, isn't it?"

"Well, yes."

"And the clerk's meddling is keeping it from you."

"It is." Erin sounded more resolute now.

"Then there's no harm in anything I intend doing. Who knows? Molly might be a Preston."

Slocum found himself with an armful of soft, curvy woman. Erin pressed her cheek hard against his chest. He felt wetness spreading as her tears spilled over.

"I'm so glad to have met you, John."

He wondered what Erin would feel when he helped himself to the gold her beau had helped steal.

"I heard tell of a new hotel opening down the street. It's actually got rooms for rent."

"Space is at such a premium in Virginia City," she said. "Can we really get rooms?"

Slocum heard how she spoke. Rooms. One for each of them. He heaved a sigh. Gold or the girl. He had to choose, and as lovely as Erin Finnigan was, she couldn't compete with ten wagonloads of gold.

"Let's go see."

They went down D Street, turned east and found the small hotel on Union a few doors down from a steepled church. This section of town wasn't as rowdy as higher on the hillside, with dozens of saloons and cribs filled with ladies of the night.

The carpenters still worked to finish the crude structure. Slocum had seen better. He had also slept in worse.

"Two rooms," he said.

"We got a waitin' list, mister," the room clerk said, but the man was staring at Erin.

"Maybe you could ease us on into the top of the list. For two rooms," Slocum said. "The lady gets the special one."

"We can do that," the clerk said, his eyes never leaving Erin. "But a second room might be a problem."

"For a member of Engine Company No. 7?"

"You a volunteer?" This broke the clerk's fascination with Erin and the way her curvaceous body filled out her dress at bosom and backside.

"Ask Sparky. He's lieutenant of the company. Or Hugh. Or Ed—"

"No need, sir. We're right proud to have anyone in the company stayin' here, leastwise for a night or two. Uh, you would work extra hard to save the hotel if there's a fire, wouldn't you?"

"That's the least I could do. I'll let Sparky know this place is special priority."

"Thank you, sir!"

Slocum was a bit surprised at how his status had changed so quickly when he invoked the name of the volunteer fire company. The clerk had treated him with a touch of veneration, as if they were fellow Masons and Slocum was a 33rd degree master.

"You go on up and rest," Slocum suggested. "I need to find a certain young ginger-haired lady."

Erin looked displeased but said nothing. The clerk hurried around the counter to help her up the steps, cautioning her that several of the planks weren't nailed into place yet. The majority of buildings in Virginia City looked to be falling down from hard use. This one was being constructed so that it might collapse at any moment, but it was better than sleeping under the stars.

Since Sparky had proven so friendly earlier, Slocum turned toward Firehouse No. 7 for a drink and to talk with his fellow firemen. The minute he entered through the swinging doors, a roar went up.

"There's our new member. Come on in, Slocum. Pull yourself up to the bar and have a beer." Sparky hurried over and greeted him. From his breath and the way he staggered a mite, it seemed Sparky had been drinking heavily most of the day.

"You off today?" Slocum asked.

"Spent most of my time in the engine house, polishin' brass and makin' sure the pumper works. We got the finest engine in the whole damn territory. And you got to do your turn, Slocum. When you comin' to the firehouse?"

"I need to wet my whistle first, and find a friend." Slocum steered Sparky to the bar. The fireman wasn't averse to letting Slocum buy him another beer.

"You got to wear this here pin." Sparky handed Slocum a heavy brass medallion the size of four silver dollars glued together, with a fire engine raised in the center and the words "Virginia City Volunteer Fire Engine Company No. 7" curling around the burnished edge. "Wear it on yer hat. Naw, that don't look right. Your coat's gotta do. This tells the world you're a member of the best damned—"

"Engine company in the territory," Slocum finished for him.

A cheer went up and Slocum found himself buying a round for all his newfound friends. It took him a couple beers to get around to asking Sparky about Molly. He had barely described her when Sparky lit up like a bonfire.

"That's one sweet-lookin' filly, yes, sir," Sparky said, beginning to slur his words from too much alcohol. "I ast after her, when you'd rode out. You said she wasn't yours and all. Heard tell she was workin' down the st-street at the Emp-emperor Saloon."

"Much obliged," Slocum said, slipping away before Sparky realized his new volunteer had left. Leaving behind the raucous cheers and off-key attempts at singing, Slocum found the Emperor at the edge of town. Like the hotel where he and Erin were staying, this had been built in the last couple days. The smell of sawdust and fresh-cut wood made his nostrils flare as he remembered riding through pine forests that stretched for scores of miles high in the Rockies. The voracious appetite Virginia City had for wood devoured trees all over the Sierras. The few stands of maple and oak he had seen outside Seamus Preston's claim had somehow escaped the savage saw that furnished endless planking for the town, probably because the veins of ore in Old Glory Canyon had played out quick.

Slocum walked into the Emperor and looked around. The noise was different here than in the Firehouse No. 7. The undercurrents were more dangerous, too. The firemen drank to have fun and break the tension of always being prepared for a fire that they all knew had to come eventually. Here the feel was more dangerous. Four gamblers worked individual poker tables and a scantily clad woman bucked the tiger at the rear of the large room, her faro rig spread out on the table in front of her.

For a moment, Slocum thought the faro dealer was Molly, but a closer look through the swirls of smoke showed him the error of that judgment. She was about the same height and had hair indistinguishable from Molly's, but she was stockier and had a hard look about her that the miners she bilked at faro never noticed.

"What's your pleasure?" asked the barkeep.

"A beer," Slocum said, "and I'm looking for a woman named Molly Preston. I was told she worked here."

"Molly Preston? Never heard of her," said the bartender. "If you're lookin' for some action, that's Matilda workin' the faro table. For the right price, you and her'd have a real good time."

"Looking for Molly," Slocum said.

"Can't help you," the barkeep said, turning away. His friendliness melted away like icicles on a summer day.

"What's a matter? Ain't she good 'nuff for the likes of you?"

For a second Slocum didn't know the man was talking to him. He did when a heavy hand crushed down on his shoulder and spun him around. Slocum reacted instinctively. As he was being whirled about, he clenched his fist and brought it in a backhand blow against the man's cheek, sending him staggering to fall across a poker table.

The gamblers jumped back, knocking over their chairs. Slocum heard the rattle as the men went for hideout guns and knives.

"You hit me," the man said, struggling to sit up on the floor amid a pile of cards and poker chips. "You son of a bitch!"

Slocum pushed his coat back so he could get to his six-shooter. His stance and the expression on his face caused the man to hesitate, but not for long.

"Nobody does that to Big Jack Montrose!"

"Well, Big Jack Montrose," Slocum said in a cold voice, "you should learn manners. It's not polite to grab a man like that."

"A man? You got nerve, mister, callin' yerself a man. You don't look like no man to me. You look like a mouse. A tiny, scared little mouse."

The Emperor Saloon went quiet as a graveyard as Slocum squared off against Big Jack Montrose. Nobody took an insult like that without a fight—or leaving town like a whipped cur.

"How scared?" Slocum's eyes never wavered. He saw sweat bead on Montrose's forehead, but the man had backed himself into a corner. He either drew down on Slocum or crawled. It was better to die than to lose face like that.

"You look real scared to me. You shit your pants yet?"

Slocum saw Montrose's hand twitch and knew the man was making his play. Faster than a striking rattler, Slocum drew his Colt Navy as he stepped forward. With his left hand he brushed Montrose's six-gun out of the way. With his own six-shooter in his right hand, he swung as hard as he could. A dull crunch of busting bone marked the impact of his barrel against the man's temple. Big Jack Montrose didn't look so big in a heap on the floor, a cut on the side of his head gushing blood like an artesian well.

"If Big Jack has any friends," Slocum said, "maybe they'd better fetch a doctor. He's going to need it."

"Never seen a man buffaloed like that before," the barkeep whispered to a customer at the bar. "The whole damn Montrose clan's gonna be madder'n wet hens over this. Big Jack was a blowhard, but he didn't deserve to get his head stove in like that."

"There are more of those belly-crawling louses?" Slocum asked. The barkeep turned as white as a bleached muslin sheet. His head bobbed up and down like it was on a spring.

"Yes, sir, there's a whole bunch of 'em. Seven, eight, never knew for sure. You'd better get on out of Virginia City 'cuz Eustace Montrose, he's not like Big Jack there. He's downright mean."

"Killed a man for lookin' at him funny," piped up the customer at the bar. "Not that I saw it, mind you. And Big Jack deserved everything you done to him."

"Think you kilt him dead," said a gambler, leaning close and looking at the fallen man. "There's gonna be hell to pay if you did."

Slocum slid his six-shooter back into its holster and settled his coat on his shoulders.

"I didn't come in here looking for trouble. I was looking for a woman named Molly. Anyone seen her?" Slocum saw no reason to keep his hunt a secret. He had asked the barkeep, and anything already said would become prime gossip in a heartbeat.

As he scanned the faces looking at him, Slocum didn't see any that showed even a hint of recognition. He had to believe Sparky had been so drunk he mistook Matilda at the faro table for Molly Preston. There was a slight resemblance, but not enough to make Slocum even want to talk to the faro dealer.

Big Jack Montrose stirred on the floor, then rolled to one side and let out a pitiful moan.

Slocum reached down, grabbed him by the collar and pulled him to his feet. Big Jack wasn't that tall. With a quick turn, Slocum pinned the wounded man against the bar.

"You think twice before you go insulting anybody," he told him. "I should have killed you, but I didn't because of the barkeep."

"What's that, mister?" The bartender looked up, startled at being mentioned.

"You offered me a free drink if I promised not to kill this pile of horse flop."

"Sure thing, mister. Here it is. Billy Taylor's Finest, straight from Kaintuck." The man's hand shook as he poured out a shot of whiskey that had never been within a thousand miles of Kentucky. But Slocum knocked it back, wiped his lips and stepped away. Big Jack Montrose slid to the floor. Hate-filled eyes glared up at Slocum.

"Who was you lookin' for?"

It took Slocum a second to realize Big Jack was speaking.

"You say you wanted to find Molly *Preston*?"

Slocum said nothing as he stared at the man struggling to sit up.

"Don't know her. Don't know any of the Preston clan." Big Jack Montrose spat in Slocum's direction but missed. The spittle, mixed with blood from a cut lip, spread out in a curious pattern on the sawdust and vanished from sight.

Slocum turned and left. He had found one of the other families involved in the robbery with Michael Preston— and it went by the name of Montrose.

12

Slocum backed away from the saloon and decided he wasn't getting anywhere asking after Molly. The woman wouldn't be far away, he thought, because he had the map and she knew it. The way she had searched his clothing after the night they'd spent in the line shack told him she was involved in the robbery up to her pretty ears. As he walked back to the hotel at the edge of town, Slocum wondered if it might not have been best if the woman had stolen the map then and there. It would have taken a considerable amount of trouble off his shoulders.

As quickly as the notion crossed his mind, Slocum ejected it. He had been duty bound to deliver the map fragment to Seamus Preston, and he had tried. It wasn't his fault someone—the Montrose gang?—had killed Seamus. But it was his choice to help Erin Finnigan. He felt she had been dealt a crooked hand. All she wanted was to keep scraping through tailings to scavenge what few flecks of color the original mine owner had missed. It was no fit life for any woman, much less one as pretty as Erin, but it was her choice.

That's what it all came down to. Choices. Slocum knew Erin wanted nothing to do with the stolen hoard of gold.

He did. Hand resting on the pocket where he kept the map, he strayed a ways to the shirt, where the half gold coin rested around his neck on the rawhide thong. He would work a deal with Erin, swapping her half of the coin that Seamus had given her for the title to the worthless mine. It felt like a swindle to him, but if both got what they wanted, who was being rooked?

The clerk had made it plain as day that he would bend all the rules for a five-hundred-dollar bribe. If Erin was right, this would be a drop in the bucket compared with the vast hoard of gold waiting for him somewhere in the mountains.

Almost back to the hotel, Slocum began to get an uneasy feeling. He turned uphill, went to C Street and sauntered past the Firehouse No. 7 Saloon but did not stop. Instead he went to the side of the raucous gin mill and stood in the shadows, waiting and watching. The street was filled with drunk miners, but he ignored them easily enough. Most only sought a new watering hole to keep them supplied with liquor until dawn, when they either returned to work or passed out.

One man wasn't drunk and he looked angry. Slocum guessed the reason. He had lost Slocum's trail. Slocum studied the man but did not recognize him. The man began a quick entry into each saloon, only to pop out when he didn't find his quarry. Slocum opened his coat and reached over to rest his hand on the butt of his six-shooter. He could draw, fire and kill the man and no one would ever notice. The very act of murder might go unnoticed until daybreak, and no one would care since Virginia City was still without a marshal. Sheriff George might be interested in hunting for anyone willing to shoot a man from ambush, but Slocum guessed the sheriff's sights were set on the Montrose gang.

And the ten wagonloads of gold that they, with the Prestons and some other family of outlaws, had made off with.

Slocum waited for his stalker to pass by. Rather than kill him, Slocum wanted information. He might even find who had the other half of the map. He wasn't going to locate the stolen gold without it, but apparently the Montroses weren't going to find it without the scrap he had.

The scrap of map and the gold coin.

That thought made Slocum less inclined to capture the man than to get back to the hotel and Erin Finnigan. Seamus had given her the half coin to hold if the Montrose gang caught up with him—as they had. The cache of food and weapons that had saved their lives must have been left by Seamus for the rest of the gang as part of his work as their quartermaster.

But this put Erin in greater danger than ever. When the gang hadn't found the coin among Seamus's belongings, they had caught him and tried to torture it out of him. Slocum wondered if Seamus had told them where the coin was before they killed him or if he had died with a tight lip.

Poking his head out to look for his tracker, Slocum waited almost a full minute before deciding the man had vanished. Either he had given up looking for Slocum and returned to report his failure to the rest of the gang, or he hadn't been tracking Slocum at all. Of the two choices, Slocum reckoned the first was closer to the truth. He had seen the man's desperation when he thought he had lost his quarry.

Slocum almost went looking for the man, then changed his mind. He kept to shadows, took alleys and eventually came out near his hotel. For several minutes, Slocum patrolled the area as he hunted for anything out of the ordinary. All he found was three miners curled up under sheets of tin, sleeping off their nightly binge.

He went into the hotel to find the clerk with his head lying on crossed arms as he slept on the counter. Slocum went up the stairs to the second floor, stepping gingerly as some of the planks were still loose. He stopped in front of

Erin's room and almost knocked. He wanted to be sure she was all right. But he held back. If she was asleep, he would worry her for no reason.

Slocum went into his room and flopped on the bed. It lacked a mattress but a couple blankets under him on the hard plank was better than sleeping on the ground. He stared at the unfinished ceiling. Lath needed to be applied, then plastered to cover the cracks. If it rained, Slocum would find himself bailing. But that was a distant possibility now with the late autumn storms being snowy rather than rainy.

He hated it that he couldn't go to sleep and that everything tumbled about until he doubted he would ever sleep. He forced himself to close his eyes. Barely had he done so when he heard a soft tread in the hallway outside his room. Someone trying not to make a sound. Courtesy was a commodity lacking in a boomtown. Slocum reached over and slid his six-gun from its holster.

His door opened a crack. Then a bulky man rushed into the room. In spite of having known this was likely to happen, the sudden attack took Slocum by surprise. He had expected a sneak thief to slip in and begin poking through his belongings. This owlhoot had come to fight.

A heavy fist missed Slocum's head and landed on his right shoulder, momentarily numbing it. He fought to keep a grip on his six-shooter, but his arm refused to obey. His fingers opened of their own accord and the gun slipped to the bed. Then Slocum found himself fighting for his life. His assailant jumped to the bed, pinned Slocum down and wrapped meaty fingers around his neck.

Slocum gagged as pressure increased to cut off his air.

The man's knees held Slocum down in a schoolboy pin, but the hard bed came to Slocum's aid. If he had been lying on a soft mattress he could never have gained enough leverage to lift his hips up, then jerk to one side. The abrupt movement dislodged the man. As he crashed heavily to the floor, Slocum went for his six-shooter. His finger curled around the trigger and discharged a round.

He missed.

Then Slocum found himself on the receiving end of more punishing blows. The man's fist landed repeatedly. If Slocum had not left on his heavy coat, he might have been beaten down and knocked out. As it was, he felt every bruising blow against his ribs and belly. He was too close to his attacker to get the muzzle of his Colt between them.

Again Slocum dropped his gun, but this time he grabbed the man's coat and yanked hard. This sent the huge man reeling back. He smashed so hard into the wall that he went through the flimsy partition and fell into the hallway.

The light was no better outside his room than it was within. Slocum couldn't get a good look at the man's face, but he didn't think it was Big Jack Montrose or even the man who had followed him through the streets of Virginia City.

With a bull-throated roar, the man got to his feet and grabbed for Slocum, preventing him from picking up his fallen six-gun. Slocum got his feet under him and heaved, lifting the man off the floor. Spinning around, Slocum staggered through the hole in the wall and heaved again. The man hit the floor and then tumbled backward down the stairs. By now the entire hotel was awake and crying out.

Slocum took a few seconds, picked up his gun and then went to finish off this annoyance once and for all. The man pulled himself to his feet. Slocum stood at the top of the stairs, aimed and cocked his six-shooter.

"Don't move," he ordered, but the man wanted none of it. Slocum pulled the trigger, and his round caught the man in the gut as he tried to charge back upstairs. The mountain of a man hung frozen for a moment, then sagged down, turned and tried to take a step. His foot went into empty space, and he fell face first to the lobby floor.

"You kilt him," the clerk said, coming from around the counter. He carried an old black-powder Remington that would probably blow up in his hand if he fired. "You can't kill guests."

"He broke into my room to steal whatever he could find," Slocum said. "He got what was coming to him."

"I guess that makes it all right," the clerk said. As he turned he swung his heavy pistol around. Slocum cried out but the clumsy clerk smashed a coal-oil lamp on the counter with the barrel. The kerosene inside spewed out across the counter. A surge of flame and a sudden blast of heat caused Slocum to throw up his hands to protect his face.

"Fire!" screeched the clerk. "Ever'body out! Fire!"

Slocum was bowled over by the rush of hotel guests trying to get away from the inferno already reaching intolerable proportions. He fell, got up and found two men grabbing his arms and dragging him out.

"Erin!" Slocum fought to get free but the men were doing what they thought was best—getting him away so he wouldn't be like a horse that runs back into a burning barn. He jerked free but another hand stopped him.

"Grab a hat and get to pumpin', Slocum. This here's what Engine Company No. 7's best at."

"There's still someone inside," he said to Sparky. The fire lieutenant shook his head and grabbed the front of Slocum's coat to hold him back.

"First, we get some water on that place. Ain't gonna do nobody no good rushin' into a fire till we got it cooled a mite."

Slocum saw the man was right. It was suicidal to enter the blazing hotel. He looked around for Erin but didn't spot her. He ran to the handle on the pumper and began working it up and down as hard as he could. In a few minutes the *chuff-chuff* of the steam engine kicked in and sent a steadier flow of water onto the blaze.

Sparky bellowed orders and got the water directed in just the right places. Seeing that the volunteers worked smoothly as a team and that his untrained presence would only slow them in their frantic effort to keep the fire from spreading to nearby buildings, Slocum went through the crowd hunting for Erin.

She was nowhere to be seen.

"Did everyone get out?" Slocum grabbed the dazed clerk and shook him to get his attention. "You started the damned fire. Did you see to it that everyone got out?"

"I guess so," the clerk said. "Didn't count. Couldn't. Too much smoke. Confusion. And you shot that fellow in the gut. That spooked me."

Slocum shoved him back, grabbed a fire ax off the engine and pulled a leather helmet down to protect his head. The fire was smoldering in what remained of the lobby, but the second story still showed signs of flame. Slocum dared not wait any longer. He dashed into the lobby and stumbled up the steps, Sparky's cries to stop not holding him back.

Using the ax to push away piles of burning debris, Slocum came to Erin's door and shouted her name.

"You in there?" Slocum used the ax to knock in the door. He knew better than to touch the brass doorknob and burn himself. The door crashed inward—and a surge of flame rocketed out to catch him in the face. His eyebrows were singed, but he turned his head to take the worst of the heat against his helmet.

"Erin!" Slocum blundered into the smoky room and looked around. The bed was empty, but the window was closed. If she had escaped, it had been into the hall and then to the street. And he had not seen her there. "Erin!"

"John," came a weak cry from the direction of the wardrobe. "Here."

Using the ax blade, he pried open the door. Cowering inside, Erin had pulled her clothing over her head. A small pitcher of water had been spilled beside her as she had used it to soak a rag to breathe through.

"We have to get out of here."

"Window was nailed shut. I tried it. The hallway. Too much fire."

"Come *on*!" Slocum dropped the ax and dragged her from the wardrobe. Erin tried to get up but lacked the strength after her ordeal. She had been trapped in a sweatbox with little enough air to breathe. Slocum scooped her up in his arms and went back to the door. The intense heat told of a rekindling on the second floor that would quickly bring the building down into charred ruin.

He kicked the door shut, turned and went to the window. The bright nailheads showed Erin had been right. Whether through oversight or downright laziness, the carpenters had kept the frame true by making sure no one opened the windows.

Slocum turned, dropped Erin on the bed, wrapped her in the blankets and then took her back into his arms.

He sucked in some air, choked on the heavy smoke and plunged through the window, twisting as he went. For a gut-wrenching second he fell, and then he crashed into the ground, Erin's weight driving the air from his lungs as she fell atop him. For a moment, Slocum lay under her, not sure what had happened. Then painful air came back into his chest and he rolled to one side, still holding her in his arms. She began struggling weakly.

"What's going on?" she asked.

"We got out," Slocum gasped out. He unwrapped her, saw she wore a nightgown and hastily wrapped her back up since Sparky and a couple others from Engine Company No. 7 were coming to see if he had been snuffed out like a flame or if he had survived.

Slocum wasn't sure how to answer if they asked. His ribs hurt like fire and every breath he took poured acid into his lungs. But Erin was safe and so was he.

Mostly.

"That's the bravest thing I ever saw," Sparky said. "About the dumbest, too. That makes you a real member of our engine company!" The fireman slapped Slocum on the back and almost knocked him over.

"She was trapped inside. Window was nailed shut, fire in the hall."

"No need to go into all that. You saved her. We ought to get you a commendation or a medal or somethin'. Mostly we stand around and piss on the fire. No offense, ma'am," Sparky said, touching the edge of his leather helmet and looking at her closely. "I do declare, Slocum, you got good taste in who you pull outta burnin' buildings."

Another volunteer shouted and Sparky ran off to tend to problems with the steam engine. The fire was about out, save for a few hot spots. The firemen went from one to the next, throwing buckets of water on them.

"You saved me, John," Erin said in a soft voice. "Nobody's ever done anything like that before. Not even Seamus."

"You didn't need saving. If you had, you wouldn't be here," he said, grinning. She wrapped her arms around him and shivered in reaction. Slocum held her but looked beyond, to the fire engine and the crowd gathered around it. The volunteers had saved Virginia City from a nasty fire that could have spread throughout most of the town. The citizens all looked on this as a great diversion from their usual night of drinking.

"I lost everything in the fire," Erin said. "All my clothes, everything."

Slocum looked down and saw his six-shooter was still in its holster. That was all he needed to get by.

"You've got more than that," he told her. "You didn't panic when the whole damned building was coming down around your ears."

"The window. I should have broken it and climbed out,

but it never occurred to me. I'm so used to thinking of glass windows as valuable, it never occurred to me. I didn't think of it." Erin began crying openly. The shock of her escape from death held her like a terrier grasps a rat in its teeth and shakes.

Slocum led her toward the engine.

Sparky came over. "Seen this a dozen times before. We got a bottle of whiskey. A shot or two'll take care of her nerves."

"Go on, give her a drink," Slocum said, but his attention was on the crowd. For a moment, he wasn't certain he saw clearly. The smoke had burned his eyes and blurred his vision. Then he was sure. Molly stood on the fringe of the crowd, her eyes fixed on him.

Slocum waved to her, but she turned and disappeared in the sea of faces.

"I'll be right back," he said. He took off at a run, got to where Molly had stood and looked around. He grabbed an onlooker's arm and spun him about. "You see a red-haired woman here a few seconds ago?"

"Naw, all I seen was you firemen puttin' out one dandy of a fire. I won twenty dollars bettin' y'all'd get it out within ten minutes. Only took you eight. Thanks!"

Slocum let him go and continued his hunt, but Molly had disappeared like water on the blaze.

13

"You got to come celebrate with us, Slocum," Sparky told him. "You're a hero. A member of Engine Company No. 7!" A cheer went up from the other volunteer firemen, but Slocum took Sparky aside. He didn't want any notoriety.

"I need to look after Miss Finnigan," he told the fire lieutenant. "You've got to see that the rest of the company's taken care of." Slocum drew out a wad of greenbacks he had been wondering what to do with since he left the Stolen Nugget Saloon back in Truckee. The scrip was worthless unless somebody happened to be traveling in the direction of the bank that had issued it, but even banknotes on a California bank could be discounted and ought to buy a couple bottles of rye.

"You need to train with us, too. You got the makin's of a great fireman. You could have my job someday."

"With you as captain?" Slocum grinned. He saw ambition written all over Sparky's face. "Where's the current captain?"

"He was the marshal. I reckon we can find a new lawman real soon but not one who's also fire captain." Sparky tilted his head to one side. He looked like some paleface Indian with soot giving him his war paint. "Our company's had a monopoly on choosin' the town marshal. You interested?"

Slocum hardly believed his ears. Sparky was offering to make him Virginia City marshal.

"Job's purty good. You get to go to all the cathouses and license the Cyprians, check the saloons to be sure the purty waiter girls all give their cut to the city coffers. Hell, saloon owners *give* you drinks. Thas why a lot of the boys like to make the rounds with the marshal."

"Sounds mighty attractive," Slocum said, "but I don't have much ambition in that direction."

"I can understand," Sparky said, nodding. "I'd do it myself, 'cept I want to concentrate on bein' the next captain of the company. Election's comin' up soon."

"Tell the men you're standing them for a round or two," Slocum said. He pointed to the wad of bills in Sparky's hand. "Consider that a contribution to your election fund."

"I knew you was a stand-up fellow, Slocum."

Sparky bellowed to the men to get the hoses drained and rolled back onto drums at the rear of the fire engine. Slocum was free to turn his attention to Erin.

"I suppose I ought to have asked Sparky for a place to stay. We could have slept in the station house."

"With a dozen men?" Erin shook her head. "I'd rather go back out to the mine and sleep in Seamus's shack."

"That's a long ride in the dark," he pointed out. "We can find a place to sleep." He eyed the ruins of the hotel and remembered the outbuilding where supplies had been stored. Arm around Erin, he guided the woman toward the shed. The side facing the hotel had charred but other than this, the structure was intact.

"This is better," Erin said. "I'm not up to riding all the way out to the claim, anyway." She sat down next to Slocum and laid her head on his shoulder. "Why does all this have to happen?"

"Because of the coin around your neck," he told her

bluntly. She jerked up and looked at him. Her blue eyes were flashing.

"What do you mean?"

He told her his suspicions about the coin. He drew out the half from around his neck and held it up, letting it spin slowly at the end of the rawhide strip.

"I took this off the back-shooter who killed Michael," he told her. "I'll bet you it matches the one you have. Fits together like peas in a pod."

Erin touched the spot between her breasts where her coin hung. She pulled it out and let it swing slowly beside Slocum's. He took hers and fitted the two together.

He had a completed coin. Peering at it in the faint starlight, he saw that her half had another scratch that looked like a lightning bolt. Then he understood. This was the compass rose and the scratch represented an N for north. The scratch on his coin indicated which direction that was. He placed the complete coin on his half of the map, oriented it and still couldn't figure where the gold cache might be. He needed the other segment of the map.

"I don't know who has the other part, but I suspect it's Eustace Montrose."

"I don't care about any of this," Erin said hotly. "It got Seamus killed, and I don't want to even *see* it." She covered her eyes like a small child denying the world around her.

Slocum was more interested. He reckoned Eustace Montrose had the rest of the map that would unlock the puzzle. Finding the outlaw might be hard, but Slocum could let the entire Montrose gang come to him. The more he considered it, the more he thought Big Jack Montrose had provoked him to get the map.

Slocum ran his finger over the sharp cut edge of the gold coin. Montrose might know Erin had the coin since it hadn't been on Seamus Preston, but she was relatively safe. However, Montrose definitely knew Slocum had half the map, but not the coin. That gave Slocum an edge. He could surrender the map, if necessary, as long as he held onto the coin.

"I need to make a copy of this," he said.

"I don't want any part of it."

Slocum folded the map and tucked it back into his pocket, but when he started to take Erin's half of the coin, she snatched it from his grip.

"Mine. Seamus gave that to me. It's all I have of his to remember him by."

"All right," Slocum said. "I promised to do what I could to get you clear title to the mine, and I'll do that. But I want the half coin, at least for a while, to fetch the gold."

"It's stolen. You shouldn't want any part of a crime like that. Seamus should never have let Michael drag him into it."

Slocum wondered how much speechifying Seamus's brother had done to persuade him. Not much, he suspected. The lure of that much gold would make even the most honest of men quake in their boots to get a piece of the pie.

Slocum lay back and noticed Erin huddled against the far wall, wanting nothing to do with him. That was fine with him. Getting involved with her would only slow him when he needed to move fast. Still, he found himself looking at the curves slowly rising and falling under the blanket as she slept. It took him quite a spell before he let sleep wash over him.

"You're makin' quite a reputation for yourself in Virginia City, Slocum," boomed Sheriff George. "I was out servin' process last night and only got back to town this morning when I heard about your darin' rescue."

"The fire?" Slocum was distracted. He had gone to the marshal's office, looking for old wanted posters. If he found Eustace Montrose's face among the pictures, he would know who wanted his map—and who wanted him dead. Slocum would have settled for a little information about the gold shipment that his map and coin promised to dump into his lap.

"What else? Fire's always worth gossipin' about. When a galoot from California not only gets hisself elected to a fire company but rescues a woman from a burnin' building, well, sir, that's the stuff of legends. You're headin' for that. Yes, sir, you are. A legend." Sheriff George's eyes flickered across the marshal's desk at the WANTED posters Slocum had laid out.

"I wondered if it was Eustace Montrose you were hunting, Sheriff. The former marshal doesn't have a WANTED poster for him or any of his gang."

"You mean any of his family." George snorted in disgust. "I declare, they're worse than the James boys over in Missouri. There was nine to ten of 'em, at least to start with. Eustace, a couple brothers, his three boys, the rest cousins or in-laws. All the product of severe inbreeding's my guess. That's the only way so many of 'em could have turned out so bad."

"They do a lot of stickups?"

"That shows you're new to the territory," the sheriff said, kicking a chair out from the corner and settling into it. He hoisted his feet to the marshal's desktop, laced his fingers behind his head and speared Slocum with his steely gaze, as if he wanted to peel back his soul layer by layer.

"I take it that the answer's yes," Slocum said.

"Them boys might have been the ones what pulled the biggest heist in Nevada Territory history. Close to a million dollars in gold."

Slocum sat without moving a muscle. This was several rows of apple trees more than he had expected.

"They weren't alone. I figured them and the Arnot boys were in cahoots. It took a powerful lot of work to make off with that much gold bullion."

"Who're the Arnot boys?"

"Don't matter. They're all dead. Found 'em, one by one, all shot dead, all 'cept one and word is that he hightailed it over the mountains to California. I reckon there was a fallin' out 'tween them and the Montrose family." Sheriff George kept his keen eyes fixed on Slocum. "Might even have been some other folks involved."

"Who might that be?" Slocum worried that the sheriff might think he had been part of the robbery when all he wanted to do was pick up the loot from it.

"Never figured that out. Might be the Arnots and these other folks, the ones I don't know, tried to do the Montroses out of their due. With that much bullion, it had to be hid out. All the lawmen were chasin' after the Montrose boys, lettin' the others do as they pleased with the gold. Nobody took it over the mountains into California or north to Carson City. I was to the south when the robbery happened, and the wagons didn't get by me."

"How about them heading east, toward Denver?" Slocum asked.

"Too many mines out that way. The smelter's on the road and them wagons didn't cut cross-country. No, the gold's hid out somewhere and Eustace Montrose and his clan are huntin' for it. My bet is that they was snookered out of it by the Arnots and are doin' all they can to find where the brothers hid it."

Slocum felt as if the map and half coin burned him. He wanted to reach over to assure himself they were still in his pocket, but he remained rock still. He knew the sheriff goaded him, probed and looked for a tell. In this high stakes poker game, Slocum was not going to lose the pot because of a hand twitch or a look that might be interpreted as him having participated in the robbery.

"Mighty strange doings," Slocum allowed.

"It surely is." The sheriff dropped his feet to the floor and stood. "I got to ride north. Some Injun trouble brewin', but it won't amount to much."

"Any word on Virginia City getting a new marshal?" Slocum asked.

"Gossip has you bein' the leadin' contender for that star. I wouldn't mind workin' with you, Slocum. You got a mean look about you that'd cow them hurdy-gurdy owners over on Sutton Avenue. You need to be mean as a rabid dog to keep them in line, yes, sir, you do. Not that keepin' them and their girls in line's my province, mind you."

"None of these gents are the Montrose or Arnot gang?" Slocum pointed to the WANTED posters.

"Nary a one. That's what makes 'em so slippery. Not many folks in these parts even know what they look like, though some, like Big Jack, annoy the hell out of everyone."

"Good hunting, Sheriff," Slocum said. He left the marshal's office, wondering how long Virginia City could tolerate not having a local lawman on duty all the time. Sheriff George dropped into town now and again, but his job lay out in the county, not within the city limits.

Slocum stepped out into the bright, clear autumn day and looked around town. Commerce was brisk and most of the miners and workers in the smelter at the foot of Mount Davidson were at their jobs. Those left in town engaged in the more normal dealings of bakeries, mercantiles, yard good stores and all the other businesses that kept a town thriving and alive.

He knew he ought to see how Erin Finnigan was dealing with the loss of all her belongings in the fire, but he steered clear of that side of town. Slocum asked after the Arnot boys, the Montroses and even hinted at the Preston brothers' role in the million-dollar robbery. He doubted Sheriff George had been entirely honest when he named such a princely sum, but everyone agreed to the size. The bankers over in California had rolled the dice and tried to ship all their ill-gained gold in one monumental shipment. Even if there had been a full company of cavalry guarding the shipment, it would have been lost. The road agents had swooped down in such strength, firing as they came, that the freighters and the guards protecting them had no chance. Of all the men caught on the wrong end of the gun that day, Slocum found only one who had survived. He was so shot up that he could hardly sit up in a chair moved to the far side of a saloon on Evans Street. Slocum bought him a drink but learned nothing from him that he hadn't known already.

After a day filled with futile effort trying to find the Montrose gang, Slocum meandered downhill and made his way to the town cemetery. He wondered if the Arnots might be buried here. Or maybe the big galoot who had tried to steal the map the night before might have been planted already. Most undertakers didn't let dead bodies pile up too long, especially ones burned badly in a fire.

Slocum found himself mighty curious to see what name was on the wood marker when he tramped into the cemetery and spotted the fresh grave. The sun was setting fast behind the mountain, so Slocum wanted to finish his business here quick and find out if Erin had settled down.

Standing at the foot of the grave, Slocum read the name on the crudely lettered cross.

"Jacob Montrose. One less of you bastards to deal with," Slocum said. Since there weren't any other new graves, he reckoned this had to belong to the man he had shot last night. In a way, the awkward clerk and the resulting fire had helped Slocum. Jacob Montrose's body would have been burned so much that Slocum's bullet wouldn't be obvious in his gut. Even if the clerk had accused him of murder, there was no one in town to report it to.

Slocum had to grin. With Sparky and the rest of the volunteer firemen going around Virginia City stirring up support for him to be the new marshal, the clerk wasn't likely ever to open his yap about the shooting. In exchange, Slocum wouldn't speak up on how the fire had started.

"He was my cousin and you kilt him."

Slocum turned cold inside. He tried to locate where the voice had come from but couldn't. "Somewhere behind him" was too vague for him to risk his life.

"Howdy, Big Jack," Slocum said, thinking he recognized the speaker. "I'm looking for your pa. Where can I find Eustace?"

"In hell!"

Slocum knew better than to remain where he stood. He feinted to his right, then dived left, sailing parallel to the ground as bullets ripped through the air where he had been. He hit the ground hard, rolled and came up with his six-shooter in hand. The darkness cloaked his attacker. Slocum stayed on his knees, not moving, waiting, watching, hoping for any clue so he could get the next—killing—shot.

"You ain't gonna kill no more Montroses!" screeched Big Jack.

Slocum swung about, saw a gnarled tree and waited until the outlaw came from behind it to finish the task he had started. Slocum leveled his barrel, then fired three times, one a little left, one a little right and one smack on target.

Big Jack Montrose let out a squeal like a stuck pig as the bullet found his worthless hide. Slocum saw the shadowy figure recoil and grab for a leg. He fired again and scored another hit. This one caught Montrose in the arm, but it failed to stop the outraged man. Montrose flopped to the ground and wiggled away until he found refuge behind a marble tombstone.

Slocum wanted to get to cover, too, but any movement in the owl-light of dusk would draw attention to him. He remained as still as a post and waited for Montrose to make a mistake.

"You killed Jacob and I'm gonna kill you, Slocum!"

Slocum corrected his aim a mite, putting his sights on the left side of the gravestone. Montrose was right-handed and would poke out from that side. Slocum only had two rounds left and had to make them count.

He fired when he saw movement, but knew instantly Montrose had duped him. The man had decoyed him with his hat.

"You're outta ammo, ain't you, Slocum? Give up and I won't kill ya. My pa wants to take you apart limb by limb. That'd make up for you murderin' Jacob."

Slocum knew exactly what was going to happen next. He saw Montrose's head rising above the tombstone, then shifted his aim back to where he had been decoyed before. Slocum knew how the man thought and anticipated his every move. Montrose had shoved his empty hat up to draw Slocum's last bullet while he fired from the side.

Slocum squeezed off his last round, then got to his feet. There had been no sound from Big Jack Montrose, and there never would be again. Slocum's bullet had stolen away the outlaw's life.

Walking over, Slocum looked down at the silent form sprawled on the grave. He kicked Montrose's gun out of his hand, just to be certain. But there was no movement.

Slocum looked at the grave where Montrose had died and laughed humorlessly when he saw the name on the marker. Pierre Arnot had preceded Big Jack Montrose to the graveyard less than a month earlier and would be waiting to greet one of the clan that had done him in.

"Burn in hell," Slocum said as he took the time to reload before heading back to Virginia City.

14

"Where you been, Slocum?" Sheriff George strode up, two deputies flanking him. Both men carried shotguns and looked as if they had eaten something that didn't set well in their bellies.

"Evening, Sheriff," said Slocum. "Nice night for taking a constitutional, isn't it?"

"Don't give me any lip," the lawman snapped. "We got reports of gunfire down at the cemetery. You wouldn't have been there and exchanged rounds with one of the Montroses, would you?"

Slocum wondered what the source of the man's information might be. The sheriff had not been too inclined to poke his nose into trouble inside Virginia City before. Why now? The lack of a town marshal had opened up licentiousness and outright crime, but not that much.

"When's it been against the law to defend yourself?"

"Was that it? Was that all you done?" Sheriff George looked as dyspeptic as his deputies. "Hand over your six-gun, Slocum. We got to go investigate this here crime."

"No crime, and I won't give you my gun." Slocum widened his stance slightly. He didn't want to throw down on the sheriff. In a way, he liked him. But that didn't mean he trusted George to take his gun when the sheriff's next act would be to heave him into the hoosegow and probably throw away the key.

"Hmmm," the sheriff said, stroking his chin. "It's all right, boys. Slocum's played square with me so far."

"Nothing's changed. Big Jack Montrose is dead back there, but he shot at me first."

"Dead, eh? No witnesses? Didn't think there would be."

"You'da kilt Big Jack yerse'f if you'd caught him, Sheriff," said the scrawnier of the two deputies. "Looks like he done you a favor."

"Saved you a bit of ammunition, if nothing else," Slocum said.

"None of your lip, Slocum."

"Was Pierre Arnot one of the family in cahoots with the Montrose gang?" he asked. Slocum saw George's reaction and knew the answer right away.

"Big Jack was pokin' round Pierre's grave?" This caught the sheriff's attention. He turned to the skinny deputy and snapped, "Get the gear. What we got in the wagon out back o' the marshal's office. Bring it all down to the cemetery. Now, damn you, and don't go lollygaggin' about, even if you see that whore you're sweet on."

"I'll go with you, Sheriff," Slocum volunteered, enjoying tweaking the lawman. If George hunted for something—the map?—he wouldn't want anyone to see what he unearthed after he dug up Arnot's grave. He obviously thought Big Jack Montrose had been intent on retrieving something from that gravesite rather than back-shooting Slocum.

"You move along, Slocum. I kin take care o' this."

"You want the shovels and picks, too?" asked the deputy.

Sheriff George pushed the man in the direction of the marshal's office, glared at Slocum, then stalked down the street with the other deputy trailing behind like a lost puppy dog. Slocum's amusement died when he realized the sheriff was intent on finding the stolen gold, too. He thought there might be something hidden in Pierre Arnot's grave that had drawn Big Jack Montrose there. Slocum wasn't so sure about that. He believed Montrose had trailed him there and thought he had a chance at murdering him and then robbing him of the map.

Slocum was glad he had never mentioned either the map or the gold coin to the lawman. He wasn't sure George was honest and wanted to recover the hoard because it was the right thing to do, or if the man wanted it all for himself. A million dollars in bullion was a mighty solid reason to abandon a dented tin star and a salary of a hundred dollars a month.

Slocum crossed town, avoiding the rowdier places but keeping a sharp eye out for anyone who might be trailing him. The sheriff was too busy digging around the cemetery, probably looking for the map. Slocum wondered if the lawman might roll Big Jack Montrose into the same grave that he opened to hunt for the map, then close the grave on the pair of outlaws. It would save them all a world of trouble since Eustace Montrose wasn't likely to take the loss of another son calmly.

Slocum doubled back a couple times but saw no one tailing him. He avoided two volunteer firemen out on the town because he didn't want to get involved in swapping drinks with them as they staggered from saloon to hurdy-gurdy to whorehouse.

His steps slowed as he approached the outbuilding behind the ruins of the hotel. Slocum wasn't sure if Erin would still be there. She had been upset with him about following the map directions and taking the stolen gold for his own. For a moment he considered how she might be right. He remembered his original distaste for the chore of taking Preston's pitiful legacy to Seamus and his outright contempt for the notion of a treasure map. That had changed since Seamus's death. Learning that the bullion had been stolen added to Slocum's yen for a golden return on what had been his sworn duty.

He stared at the closed door, then reached out, took the rope loop that served as a handle and opened it.

A gasp came from inside.

"Sorry," Slocum said, but he wasn't that sorry. Erin was dressing. Her blouse hung open, revealing her luscious breasts. Her legs poked out from under a too-short skirt, giving Slocum a clear view from her ankles all the way up to her thighs.

"See you got some clothes."

"Either come in or leave. Whatever you do, close that door," Erin said irritably.

"Which would you prefer?" Slocum asked.

The dark-haired woman started to speak, then paused, considered, and a slow smile came to her lips.

"In," she said. "Please come in and shut the door behind you."

Slocum did as Erin bid, then sank down beside her on the blanket he had pitched the night before.

"Where did you get the clothes?" he asked.

"Your friends in the fire engine company. They took up a collection." Erin actually blushed. "They went up and down Union and D Streets asking."

Slocum knew these streets were where the cribs and brothels were most likely to be found. Sparky and the rest of the volunteer firemen had solicited spare clothing from whores for Erin. That she had accepted showed how desperate she had been.

"I didn't know when they gave them to me, but I'm so ashamed, John. After I found out, I didn't want to give them back."

"You could have walked around Virginia City naked," he said.

"That would have been a pretty sight," she said, getting her dander up again.

"Yes, it would," Slocum said quietly.

"I've got so much to be embarrassed about," Erin said, her eyes not meeting his. "You saved my life last night. Everyone says so. And when you asked for the gold coin, I got mad. It's not that unusual that you'd want to find the gold Seamus and the rest stole. I never asked if you were going to return it for the reward."

"No, you didn't," Slocum said. He was glad she hadn't. He would have been honest and told her he wanted it all for himself and made her really angry. He hoped she wouldn't now since he wouldn't lie to her now, either. It was one thing making off with gold already stolen. It was another matter entirely lying or going back on your word.

"The clothes don't fit too well, do they?" she asked. She looked up with her blue eyes gleaming. A faint smile danced on her ruby lips again, and she leaned back slightly, bracing herself on her hands and drawing up her knees. "I suppose I ought to take them off."

"After just putting them on?" Slocum saw what was on her mind, and it had occurred to him, too, the instant he opened the door and saw her. She was one fine-looking woman. He felt himself responding to the banter, until it got downright uncomfortable being in his jeans.

"I'm not used to these things," Erin said. "Why don't you help me get out of them?"

Slocum bent over and reached for the blouse, to move it away from her shoulder. Erin batted his hand away. He looked at her in surprise.

"Don't use your hands," she said. Her voice had turned husky, and her eyelids drooped to half-mast. When she shoved her chest out and let the blouse flop open to expose her succulent, snowy white breasts, Slocum got the idea.

This time as he bent forward, he supported himself on

his hands and used his teeth to worry back the cloth from her shoulder. He kissed lightly as he went and occasionally let his tongue dart out to touch spots he thought would be most sensitive. His instincts were unerring. Every wet lick of his tongue caused a new ripple of desire to pass through the woman's body.

"This is what I like most, John. Your mouth. Your mouth and lips and tongue everywhere, all over my body."

Slocum couldn't answer because his mouth was occupied with stripping her blouse off. He had finished with one arm and worked the blouse down over the other, to leave Erin sitting on the blanket, naked to the waist. In the faint light of the rising moon filtering in through cracks in the walls and roof, her skin turned to liquid silver. But no metal had ever been so soft, tender and seductive.

He brushed lightly over one nipple and then the other. They tasted salty as he suckled and then nipped with his teeth. His tongue shot out and crushed the hard nub down into the softness below. Erin groaned and sank back to lie on the blanket. Her strength had fled as Slocum kept up his oral assault on her body.

He slid down the steep slope into the deep valley between to lavish more kisses her. He pushed aside the double eagle coin segment he found there. It would have been easy to snare it in his teeth, yank and win it as his prize. But Slocum wanted something more now.

Slipping from side to side, he went lower and lower across her belly. He paused a moment to dip into the deep well of her belly button, but this wasn't his goal. His tongue whirled about like a tornado and came to the tight waistband of her skirt. Here Slocum started to cheat, to use his fingers to release the button.

Again Erin stopped him.

"No," she said. "Teeth. Rip off the button!"

He was not going to gainsay her. His teeth locked around the large button holding together the skirt, and then he reared back, tossing his head like a magnificent stallion. The thread yielded, the button pulled off and Erin's skirt flopped open. He pounced on it like a mountain lion going after a rabbit. Using only his teeth, he pulled and harried and finally dragged the offending skirt away from the aroused woman's middle, to expose the spot he most wanted to sample.

"Yes, there, do it, John. I want it so!"

His lips kissed the heaving dome of her belly and then glided directly lower to the top of her pink nether lips, where he found a tiny bud growing. He licked and sucked and kissed and then drew it into his mouth as far as he could.

Warm thighs crushed down powerfully on his ears and held him at his post. He realized Erin had reached the breaking point. He thrust out his tongue and slid from the quivering button of flesh into the woman's moist interior. He began a steady motion that lifted Erin's hips off the blanket and ground her crotch hard into his face.

Slocum's tongue began to tire, but the woman showed no signs of wanting him to leave. He surfaced for air, turned and lightly nipped her inner thigh. This set off a new tremor that passed through her trim body like an earthquake.

As her legs parted this time, Slocum moved between them and up on her body. He kept licking and kissing, but now he was struggling to get himself out of his pants. He succeeded and released the fierce, hard length that had been trapped for too long.

Before Erin could protest, he kissed her full on the lips, slid an arm under her left knee and lifted so her ankle rested on his shoulder. Tiny animal noises came from her now. Her eyes were clamped shut in ecstasy, and she tossed her head from side to side as the sensations rippling through her body built in intensity once more.

She cried out in rapture as Slocum moved his hips,

knocked on the gates to her inner fastness, then rushed inside. He gasped when he felt himself surrounded by her moist warmth. For a frenzied heartbeat, he paused, relishing the crush of her heated flesh around his. He withdrew slowly, savoring every inch of the retreat until only the thick head of his manhood remained with her.

Ankle still on his shoulder, he bent forward again and entered her more slowly this time. The contrast between his first all-out thrust and this slow invasion caused her breasts to rise and fall rapidly, delightfully, as she gasped for breath. He kept up the agonizingly slow thrust and retreat until he wondered how he could stand even another instant of it. His loins were ablaze with need. He felt the hot white tide building inside and fought to contain it.

He wanted as much of this stark, animal pleasure as possible. But Erin foiled him. She reached up and stroked his face, his cheeks, his lips, thrust her finger into his mouth. Then her knowing hands moved down his hirsute chest—and surged lower. Her teasing fingertips danced lightly on one of the tight, hard spheres dangling beneath his erect shaft. It was as if she had dipped her fingers in acid. Every touch sent shocks through him.

Slocum grunted, ducked his other shoulder to scoop up her right leg and draped that ankle over his shoulder. Bent double, she could only accept his every move. Her upper legs pressed down hard into her breasts and crushed them flat. His stalk buried deeper and deeper into her until Erin cried out in release once more.

This was more than Slocum could stand. He fought to hold back his own ultimate pleasure and could not. Sliding forward as far as possible into her core, he split apart and spewed forth his load. He lost all sense of time and place as he moved, friction heating his entire length and giving him the ultimate in human pleasure.

Spent, he released her legs to fall on either side of him. He put his head down on her breasts for a moment, then rolled to the side. Erin's arms curled around him as she clutched him tightly.

"Is it always this good?" she asked.

"Gets better," Slocum assured her.

"Oh?" Erin pushed back and looked at him sternly. "You'll have to prove that!"

"Later," he said.

"Not much later, I trust," she said, but she returned, to put her head against his chest and listen to his strong heartbeat.

Content for the moment, Slocum lay with his arms around her and let his thoughts tumble and flow in odd directions. No matter how he remembered the lusty coupling with Erin, thoughts of gold always intruded. He found himself in the same situation as Eustace Montrose. He had half the map and all of the double, and it still didn't tell him where the gold was stashed. Whoever had thought up the system had wanted to be certain no one sneaked back to get the loot without the others along. Slocum had three-quarters of the information and was as far from getting the gold as Montrose.

Working a deal with the outlaw and his cutthroat family hardly seemed likely. Montrose had slaughtered all his partners in the crime. Both Prestons were dead, as well as the Arnot family. Dealing with such a hardcase was out of the question, unless it was with a six-shooter pointed at the man's gut.

Even then Montrose might prefer to die rather than cut in someone outside his family.

"John," came an urgent whisper. "John, are you in there?"

Slocum sat bolt upright and grabbed for his six-gun. He disturbed Erin out of her light sleep. She rolled over and clutched at the blanket in a fit of unnecessary modesty.

"What's wrong, John?" Erin sat up and began grabbing for her too-small clothing.

"I heard Molly calling. From outside." Slocum hastily pulled on his clothes, making sure to settle his cross-draw holster properly so he could get to his six-shooter if necessary.

Erin took a bit longer to complete her toilet. She scrambled to her feet when Slocum opened the door and peered into the darkness.

"What do you see?"

"Nothing," Slocum said. "I wasn't imagining it. I heard her."

"Does she need your help?" Erin's tone carried a mixture of anxiety and anger. "How'd she know you were here?"

That thought had crossed Slocum's mind already. He drew his six-shooter and pulled open the door a bit farther to poke his head out for a quick look. He saw a faint figure on the far side of the burned down hotel that might have been Molly Preston. She waved to him, then walked away.

"Wait!" Slocum stepped out of the shed, still cautious of a trap. "Molly!" She kept walking, never looking back. Slocum found himself caught between running after the elusive woman and remaining with Erin.

"Hurry, John," came the distant plea. "Hurry."

"Don't leave me," Erin pleaded. She clung to his arm but he pulled free.

"I need to talk to her. She might know where the rest of the map is. If not, she certainly knows more about what's going on than either of us."

"No!"

Slocum ignored Erin and plunged into the chilly night. To the north lay Virginia City, bright and bawdy. To the west rose a steep slope to the top of Gold Hill, and south were more mines than he could count. Molly headed in that direction.

"Molly!" His cry fell on deaf ears. He saw her walking at a steady pace but rapidly widening the distance between them. Slocum broke into a lope that devoured the ground and brought Molly more clearly into view. Then he skidded to a halt when he heard Erin shriek in fright. On the heels of that anguished cry came a bass laugh that rumbled like thunder through the still night.

Slocum watched as Molly disappeared around a bend in the road, then reversed his course and dashed back to the outbuilding, cursing himself for being lured into a trap—but not for him. For Erin. He kicked open the door to the shed and thrust his Colt Navy in before him.

Empty. The shed was empty save for a scrap of paper on the blanket where he and Erin had just made love.

Slocum picked up the paper and read the few words on it. Eustace Montrose had Erin. He didn't have to say that he would kill her unless Slocum turned over the map. That was unstated.

So was how Slocum was supposed to exchange the map fragment for the woman's life. Eustace had not wasted ink on such details. All Slocum could do was wait.

That wasn't something he wanted to do with Erin's life on the line.

15

Slocum wasn't the sort to sit around and do nothing. He knew Eustace Montrose expected him to stew and churn in his own juices, so that when a demand note came to ransom Erin Finnigan, he would obey frantically and without question. Instead, Slocum let a cold anger possess him.

With that anger came an even colder logic. Molly had lured him away. He had not seen anyone who might have been a Montrose with her, holding a gun to her head or forcing her to obey. That meant Molly and the Montrose gang were in cahoots. In a way, Slocum preferred it this way. He didn't have as many loose ends to tie up. With Molly and Eustace Montrose looking for the same thing— the map—Slocum stood a better chance of eliminating them all at once. And if, as he suspected, Montrose had the last part of the map, he might stir a little dissension in their ranks by turning Molly against the Montrose family. How hard could that be? They all wanted to be sole owners of a million dollars' worth of gold bullion ripped from the mines around the Comstock Lode before even more silver had been discovered.

Slocum looked in the direction Molly had taken and knew he could never follow her in the dark. Instead, he dropped to his knees, struck a lucifer and studied the ground around the shed until the match burned his fingers. He dropped the burnt match and set off in the direction of the tracks leading away from the outbuilding. The steep hill quickly leveled off into a rocky field. He found where Montrose had left his horses. From the tracks, Slocum guessed there had been three others with him. Two sons and a spare horse for Erin? To Slocum's surprise they had ridden south, possibly to join up with Molly somewhere along the road.

Returning to the shed, Slocum fetched his horse, saddled and mounted. He might overtake them if Montrose thought he was safe and rode slowly, but Slocum didn't count on that. The moonlight was bright enough to track by, but gathering clouds often obscured it and cast long, deep shadows across the ground.

Spurring his horse to a trot, Slocum returned to the area where Montrose had left his horse, then began the tedious process of tracking in the dark using only the hide-and-seek moonlight to work by. About an hour before dawn, bone-tired and almost falling out of his saddle from exhaustion, Slocum spotted the Montrose clan's campsite.

He sat astride his horse, sizing up the opposition. He knew he could ride in, shooting anyone who moved. If he did that, though, Erin might be killed in the confusion. Slocum doubted Eustace Montrose had much control over his family, other than to bully them. This wasn't a disciplined cavalry troop but a gang of greedy outlaws each wanting a mountain of gold bars stacked in front of him.

Greed made for stupidity.

As he pondered that, Slocum almost laughed aloud. He was getting greedy and he was getting stupid. He had to play this hand right to keep Erin from getting killed—and still rake in the biggest pot of all. A million dollars in gold was a powerful goad.

Sheriff George might be called in, but Slocum knew the

outcome of that. The sheriff wanted the gold for himself. Slocum smelled the greed boiling from the man's pores every time the gold was mentioned. If involving the lawman was foolish, not being able to attack straight on was out of the question, and waiting for Eustace Montrose to deliver a ransom note played into the owlhoots' hands and wrote a death sentence for both Erin and himself—that left only one course of action.

Slocum slid from the saddle, poked around in his saddlebags until he found his spare Colt and tucked it into his gunbelt. He could sneak as good as any Indian and intended to prove it. It was still too dark to be sure where everyone slept in the camp, but Slocum doubted the Montrose gang would be wary of him coming. If anything, they'd be passing around a bottle, celebrating how easy it was to put one over on the interloper—and how they were going to divvy up the gold and spend it when they got the map from him.

Tethering his horse some distance away, where if it whinnied it would not draw attention, Slocum checked his firearms and began the slow descent into the camp. He watched for lookouts, but saw none. He relied on a silent tread and kept to the shadows to get within fifty feet of the camp. In the middle of the camp blazed a fire that cast flickering light across the terrain and the four large, old Army tents that had been pitched. Slocum tried to get one tent between him and the fire to see if he could make out silhouettes inside. With luck, he could see where Erin was being held.

Or Molly. The difference in what he would do was simple when it came to the auburn-tressed beauty. He would gladly plug her for luring him away so Erin could be kidnapped.

The canvas in the tents proved too thick for him to get a good idea of who was inside any of them. He saw two men sitting on rocks near the fire, huddled over and not talking. They drank silently. In the ten minutes he watched them, they poured themselves two cups of coffee from a pot boiling on the fire. Slocum suspected they also added a hefty dollop of whiskey to their coffee before drinking it, but both men were cast in heavy shadow from where he spied.

He watched and waited another half hour before anyone came to join the pair at the fire. The man who crawled from one of the tents stood up and might have been a grizzly bear decked out in human clothing. He was immense, broad of shoulder and with a belly that bounced every time he took a step. Slocum knew better than to discount the man, however, because of the way he carried himself. He might look fat, but the quickness of his movement told of great strength. He looked like a bear and might be able to crack a man's back with his own version of a bear hug.

"You boys ain't all liquored up now, are you?" The man walked around and grabbed a tin cup from one man's hands. He lifted it and took a deep whiff. "I thought so, you drunken sots! No sons of mine'll disobey me when I tell 'em to stay sober. Who's out there watchin' for that sneaky son of a bitch Slocum?"

"Aw, Pa, he ain't gonna come after that skinny little whore. She ain't got much meat on her bones. Not like Essie May."

"You ain't got the brains God gave a goat. It don't matter what *you* like in a whore. It matters what *he* does. If Slocum's sweet on her, he won't want her all cut up."

"We could use her a mite and see what he likes 'bout her," suggested the other man. The giant cuffed him so hard it knocked him off the rock where he had perched like some carrion eater.

"The both of you. Stupid! If brains was gunpowder you couldn't blow your own noses."

"Why'd we want to—" The first man ducked as the mountain of a man swung at him.

Slocum remained as quiet as a statue, watching, taking it all in, getting ready to act. He pegged the huge man as

Eustace Montrose and the other two as his remaining sons. Nobody had ever said exactly how many sons Eustace had riding with him, but it was a family affair, with his brothers and a couple cousins, too. But the Arnots had not died without putting up a fight. Any of them might have taken out a Montrose, and Michael Preston's killer had some of the facial features of the unlamented Big Jack Montrose. Eustace was losing his family one by one and didn't much care.

All that mattered was the gold.

"You worthless worms have one thing right. Might be downright interestin' to find out what she's got to entice a man like Slocum." Eustace started for the tent on the south side of camp, then paused. He tilted his head to one side, sniffed the air like a bloodhound and turned slowly in a full circle.

"What's wrong, Pa?"

"Don't know. There's somethin' not right. You get out there and keep an eye peeled."

"I don't unnerstand why you're expectin' him to come here. How would he find us? Wasn't he supposed to wait back in town till you gave him another note? A ransom note with instructions?" The man stumbled over such big words. Slocum thought he was repeating what he had heard someone else tell him.

"He's too antsy for that. If he don't find us, then I'll send him a note. But he's not like you, Teddy. He's smart."

"Pa, that's not right, raggin' on Teddy like that."

"The both of you get your asses out there and watch for Slocum. Me, I think I'll go get myself bedded down for a spell." Eustace Montrose laughed, hitched up his trousers and went to the tent to his right.

Slocum wondered where Erin was being held. From Eustace's first words, he thought she might be in the southernmost tent, but he had gone to the one on the west side of the camp. Slocum went cold inside thinking of this animal forcing himself on Erin.

If he had half the sense Eustace Montrose credited him with having, he would bide his time and permanently remove the two sons from their lookout posts. It never paid to have an armed enemy at your back. But Slocum couldn't take the time. He heard a soft female moan from inside the tent where Eustace had gone. The objection grew louder, then was cut off when the man obviously used a big, loud kiss to silence any further protests.

Thrashing sounded inside the tent and galvanized Slocum. He threw caution to the winds and raced to the tent. A quick look around showed that Montrose's sons had not heard the brief clatter of boots against rock. They might have been too drunk to notice anything less than falling over a cliff.

Slocum drew back the tent flap and poked his six-shooter inside.

"Get off her, Montrose," he said coldly. "Get off her or I'll ventilate your worthless, flea-bitten hide."

In the dim light all Slocum could see was a white leg drawn up and Eustace Montrose with his pants down around his ankles. Opening his fly was what passed for foreplay with him, but what else did he need for rape?

The huge man looked over his shoulder at Slocum, startled. Then he laughed.

"I'll be switched. He's here to save your honor, little miss."

"Get off her so I can blow your worthless balls off and serve 'em to you like Rocky Mountain oysters," Slocum said. "If you—"

Montrose moved and Slocum saw the woman in the bed for the first time. Molly kicked out and knocked the six-gun from his grip. Then he found himself mixing it up with a half-naked Eustace Montrose. The man was as immensely strong as he had suspected and faster. Much faster. Slocum's only advantage lay in Montrose having his pants down around his hairy ankles.

Slocum clapped both of his palms against the sides of Montrose's head, crushing his ears. Montrose growled like a beast and tried to grapple. Slocum kicked out and caught a knee, knocking the man down, but this was almost his undoing. The tent was small and restricted Slocum's movement. He felt a meaty paw of a hand clamp down like a vise on his leg.

A quick yank brought him crashing to the ground.

"Never corner anyone meaner than you, John," Molly said, gloating. "Don't kill him, Eustace. We need the map."

"If he's got it on him, I'll take it. If he don't, I'll strip his hide off inch by inch till he tells me where it is."

Slocum twisted hard and kicked Eustace Montrose in the face. For a moment, he didn't think he had done any damage. Then, as if it took the monster of a man a couple seconds to realize he was injured, Montrose let out a bellow of pure pain and rage. Slocum had smashed the man's nose amid a shower of blood.

Scrambling to get his feet under him, Slocum heard a sound that was all too familiar. A gun had cocked. He looked at the bedding and saw a naked Molly sitting crosslegged, his own gun pointed at him. She held it steady in a two-handed grip, but there was no doubt that she could hit him at this range.

"The map, John. Give me the map."

"It won't do you any good."

"It'll be a damn sight better than letting you keep it."

"You've already got the other half?"

"No more talk. The map or I see how many times I can hit you before you die."

Eustace Montrose still moaned and pressed his hand into his fountaining broken nose. Slocum slumped as if in resignation, then jumped sideways. He crashed into the pole supporting the tent and brought it down just as Molly shot. The slug ripped past his shoulder and drilled a neat hole in the thick canvas.

Then Slocum was twisting, turning, dodging and making his way toward the tent at the south end of camp. Molly was cursing but nowhere near as loudly as Eustace Montrose. The canvas flapped like some giant flightless bird trying to soar aloft, but it held them as surely as ropes might have.

Slocum dragged his other Colt from his belt and was swinging it when the flap on the southernmost tent opened. His barrel caught the bearded man squarely on the chin. Slocum saw the older man's eyes roll up in his head before he folded like a bad poker hand.

Stumbling over the man's prone body, Slocum burst into the tent. Erin Finnigan lay all trussed up on a bedroll. When she saw him, she tried to cry out in joy but a gag had been savagely crammed into her mouth. She began choking, until Slocum ripped it out.

"Oh, John. Thank you. We've got to get out of here. There're eight of them. And . . . and that Molly woman. She's in cahoots with them.

She—"

"Never mind," Slocum said. "I know most of it already." He slid the knife from the top of his boot and slashed at the rough hemp rope binding her. She sagged as he cut her hands free, then rubbed circulation back. He made quick work of the ropes on her ankles.

"No time for that. Come on." Slocum went to the back of the tent and drove the point of his knife into the canvas. He sliced downward with a deft stroke and grabbed Erin by the hand. He pulled her behind him through the cut, and they headed into the dwindling darkness to the south of the Montrose gang's camp.

"Where are we going?" panted Erin. She stumbled repeatedly and Slocum was tiring of dragging her along behind him.

"We have to get around to where I left my horse. There's no way we can outrun them on foot. We're running out of time fast." Dawn turned the far horizon pink with the promise of a new day. Or was it the curse of a day filled with his and Erin's deaths?

"Pa, over here! I hear them over in this direction!" The words rang clarion clear. A bullet followed them that forced Slocum to duck in spite of himself. He hadn't thought either of Eustace's sons would be that good a shot in the dark. It was even worse if it had been a lucky shot. Sometimes luck is better than skill. He couldn't count on them turning unlucky or his own luck improving.

"This way," Slocum whispered. He bent low and worked his way toward some brambles. Erin let out an involuntary yelp when one raked her skin and left behind a bloody trail.

He shoved her flat on the ground, cocked his six-shooter and waited. Slocum didn't have to bide his time long. One outlaw came blundering through the woods, his nose working like his old man's had back in camp. Slocum wondered if they were crossbred with dogs. Then he got a clean shot and took it.

The man stiffened, tried to raise his rifle and finally toppled backward to lie kicking on the ground.

"You got him!" cried Erin. Slocum clamped a hand over her mouth, but she struggled. "Stop that."

He should have warned her more sternly about making noise. He saw two more of the Montrose clan closing in on them.

"I'll decoy them after me. You wait until they're on my tail, then you head to the north of the camp. Get my horse and fetch Sheriff George."

"But you—"

"No arguing," he said harshly. He hated telling the woman to get the lawman, but he had no choice. He might have to give up hope for finding the million dollars in bullion, but regretting it the rest of his life was better than getting murdered by these kidnapping no-account sidewinders right now.

Or letting them catch Erin again.

"John, please."

"Stay low until I'm out of sight, then run like hell." He didn't wait to hear any more argument from her. Slocum aimed carefully and fired. He hit another of the Montroses but did not kill him outright. If anything, winging him made the man madder than a wet hen—and far more dangerous.

Slocum crashed through the undergrowth, making as much noise as he could before turning stealthy like a stalking Apache. He flopped on his belly and slid through the tall grass like a snake, trying not to stir the vegetation too much. When he got to a stand of trees not far off, he chose a sturdy-looking maple and clambered up it to lie flat along the lowest limb. This put him just above head level for most men and gave him a good view of his backtrail.

His heart almost exploded when he saw the man he had wounded come into sight. The man hesitated before entering the wooded area, though. Slocum fingered his gun and wondered if he dared to shoot again. He decided against it. Better to jump down like a pouncing cougar and finish off the son of a bitch with his knife. He didn't want to attract too much attention, though he might have to if he wanted to give Erin a decent start toward reaching his horse and safety.

"Uncle Paul, that you in there?" The man swung his rifle around in a short, nervous arc that told Slocum he was still searching for a target. "Uncle Paul?"

Slocum worried that Uncle Paul would show up, but instead the man retreated and went back toward camp. Slocum wasn't sure if he was lucky or not. He wanted to eliminate as many of the Montroses as he could and keep them off Erin's trail.

Swinging down, Slocum dropped lightly to the ground

with every intention of shooting his tracker in the back if he had to. He froze when he heard a ruckus from the direction of the camp. Shots sounded, then loud cries went up.

Through the still of the night he heard Molly's shrill voice.

"We got her, Slocum. We caught the poxy whore. And we got your horse, too. It was staked out north of camp. You got ten seconds to show your face or we start with her."

"I get her first," came Eustace Montrose's words, muffled and almost unrecognizable since Slocum had mashed his nose. "And after my boys and brothers and their sons have had their way with her, I'll finish her off. You won't recognize her, Slocum. She'll look like a side of carved-up beef. I'm real good with a knife. Like a Sioux, they tell me."

"Unless you show yourself and give us the map," finished Molly.

Slocum knew when he was beaten. He couldn't run and leave Erin to such a fate. But if he tried dealing with the Montrose gang, he was likely to end up dead himself.

He had no choice. Slocum called out, "I'm on my way down. Don't touch her!"

Then he started for the outlaws' camp like he was walking up the steps to the gallows for his own hanging.

16

"We kin kill her slow or we kin kill her fast, Slocum," called Eustace Montrose. "But we don't want to do any of that. Not if you give us the map."

"You've got it, John. I know you do," said Molly. "You could have avoided all kinds of tussle with us if you'd let me steal it."

Slocum noticed how Molly referred to herself as one of the Montrose clan. It made sense in a peculiar way. She and Eustace were sweethearts, and she had probably gotten involved with him because she had been unable to get the map on her own. A cut of a million dollars was better than nothing, even if it meant bedding down with the likes of Eustace Montrose. Slocum still couldn't figure if she really was a Preston or if she was someone who had happened along and decided to deal herself into the biggest game ever played in Nevada Territory. No matter what Molly was, her status did nothing to get him out of the pickle he found himself in now. Eustace Montrose had Erin and would undoubtedly do everything he had promised to her if Slocum didn't deliver the map.

"All right," Slocum shouted. "I'll let you have the map, but not if you've harmed one hair on Erin's head."

"We could scalp her 'fore we kill her, Pa," piped up one of the younger Montroses. "That'd be a whale of a lot o' fun."

"You see how it is with my boys, Slocum? They're quite a handful. Don't rightly know how much longer I kin keep 'em from doin' all this nasty stuff to your purty l'il friend."

Erin shrieked in pain. Slocum didn't have to see her to know one of the Montrose gang had probably stuck her with a knife or done something even worse to squeeze such a cry from her.

"I said I'm coming," Slocum called. "You go harming her and you'll wish you hadn't." He silently added, *No matter what you do, you'll wish you'd never crossed me.*

He skidded and slid down the steep slope and finally came out a dozen paces away from the campfire. Eustace and his boys were looking in the wrong direction, expecting him to come from a different angle. Only Molly stared directly at him. Guessing who the brains of this gang was proved easier by the second. Slocum had to deal with Molly, not Eustace. She probably had him wrapped around her little finger.

"Here it is," Slocum said, holding up the map so they could see it.

"How do we know that's it?" asked Eustace Montrose. "Get yer ass on over here with it so we kin give it a good lookin' over."

"John, don't. Don't give it to them. They'll kill us both when you do." Erin was knocked to the ground by a back-handed slap delivered by Molly.

"Don't know what you see in her, John," Molly said. "She's skinny and she talks too damn much. Can't possibly be as good between the blankets as I am."

Slocum advanced slowly, map catching the faint night-time wind. He had one chance only and had to take it.

"Gimme," Eustace said.

Slocum held out the map, then ducked under the giant's

outstretched hand and dived for the fire. As he rolled past the fire pit, he grabbed a smoldering twig. Slocum came to his feet and whirled about. He held the smoking stick close to the map.

"I can set fire to it before you can drop me. Get your boys—the ones with the rifles—back into camp, Montrose." His words were directed to Eustace but his eyes were fixed on Molly.

"Do as he says, dearie," Molly said. "He's an honest man. Or as honest as any you're likely to find in this god-forsaken place. If he says he'll let her die and himself, too, but burn up that there map, he means it."

Slocum moved the twig about in the air, fanning the slumbering coals along its length. A tiny fire leapt from the tip, as if some demon from hell had sent the flame. Slocum moved the branchlet closer to the map. From the set of his jaw, Molly and Eustace saw he was not joking about setting fire to the map.

"We get to ride out of here. You get the map, and we keep our lives," he said.

"John, honey, you oughta know I don't mean you no harm." Molly's words carried more than a touch of irony. "You jilted me for her, you done 'bout ever'thing you can think of to keep me from what's rightfully mine, you even shot up one or two of Eustace's boys, but I don't hold none of it against you. Really, I don't."

"Horses," Slocum said. "Mine and another for Erin."

"Now, John, we ain't gonna give you a horse. You two ride out together on what brung you here."

"Is a minor point like that worth watching a million dollars in gold go up in smoke?" Slocum moved the burning twig under the map. Brown splotches appeared as it scorched.

"Give him the damn horse, Molly," Eustace cried. But Slocum saw that the woman remained adamant. It was going to be her way or know the reason why.

"Your life worth that sheet of paper? Your life and hers, too?" Molly jerked her thumb in the direction where two of the gang held Erin between them. She sagged but her eyes were open and her expression showed nothing but utter hatred for the outlaws. Slocum found something else to agree with Erin over.

"Bring my horse," he said. "Then pile your guns in that tent." He pointed to the one where Erin had been held captive. "I'll drop the map as we ride off."

"Now, why should we trust you?" Molly enjoyed the battle of wits too much for Slocum to feel easy. He was overlooking something but didn't know what it might be.

"If you want the map, that's the way you'll get it. You said honesty was a failing of mine. I promise to drop the map when you let us ride out."

"Not in the fire?" Molly continued to probe the limits of his truthfulness.

"Not in the fire," he agreed with some reluctance. That had been his plan. Mount, ride past the fire and drop the map. The added scramble to pull it from the flames would have given him and Erin another few seconds' head start. Slocum wasn't fooling himself into thinking Montrose would just let them ride off scot-free. Once he had the map, he would take revenge for the sons Slocum had plugged.

"Fetch his horse," Molly ordered.

"Erin," Slocum called. "How many were in the camp?"

"They're all here," she said. "The ones that are still alive."

Slocum wished she hadn't tried to hit back at Montrose with that verbal jab. It only added fuel to the man's hatred. Then Slocum decided it hardly mattered. Montrose could hate him a little or a lot. The result would be the same either way.

"Let her go." Slocum wanted this over fast. The twig

was turning to ash, and soon enough he wouldn't have an easy way of ransoming the woman. "Let her get mounted."

"Boys, be gentlemen fer a change," Molly said. "Help her onto Slocum's horse. Back of the saddle so he kin ride all natural-like."

Slocum saw the two holding Erin drag her to the horse and then boost her so she straddled the horse's rump. He didn't like the way they grabbed Erin's rump as they helped her up, but he said nothing. His first chore was to get the hell out of camp.

He walked to the horse, checked to be sure they had piled their rifles and six-shooters in the tent as he had demanded, then he flew into action. Two quick steps and a swift kick knocked the pole down on the tent, covering the weapons and forcing the gang to dive beneath the canvas for them. Then he dropped the firebrand, crumpled the map and tossed it as hard as he could out of camp into the night. The balled-up map didn't go far, but it held their attention long enough for him to get his foot in the stirrup and pull himself up into the saddle. Before he got a good seat, his heels were raking the horse's flanks to get it moving into the night.

Then Slocum let out a yelp of surprise as the saddle shifted under him suddenly. He tried to hold on to the horse's mane but was already too far unbalanced to one side. He crashed to the ground with Erin right behind him.

"They cut the saddle strap," he said, scrambling to get his feet under him. He grabbed Erin's arm and pulled her erect—and looked down the barrel of Eustace Montrose's rifle.

"That Molly o' mine, she's sure a smart one, ain't she?" Montrose motioned for Slocum and Erin to precede him back into the camp, where the entire gang huddled around Molly, who had smoothed out the crumpled map and was piecing it together with one she already had.

"This will tell us ever'thing we need to know, Eustace," she said excitedly. "Git rid of them. Permanent-like. I want to watch."

"Don't want to rush things with 'em," the huge outlaw said. A feral smile curled his lips. "I know jist the way to take care of 'em, the way they deserve to be took care of."

After Eustace explained, even Molly was enthusiastic.

"How deep do you reckon it is?" Molly looked over the lip of the pit. She tossed a stone over. The echo of it hitting water came back after way too long for Slocum to be comfortable.

"What's the difference? A mile or ten?"

"I like it you don't wanna kill 'em off right away. In case there's a problem with the map."

"I don't wanna kill 'em fast at all. You said the map was all we needed. Ain't that so?" Eustace looked at Molly with a spark of anger in his piglike eyes.

"We got all we need to find the gold them Arnots hid on us."

"Them and those two worthless, good-for-nuthin' Preston brothers. They was in cahoots."

"Jist like we are, honey," Molly said, cozying up to Eustace. "Wasn't the robbery my idea? How'd I know Michael and Seamus would get greedy?"

"Seamus was a better man than any of you!" shouted Erin. For her trouble she got a strong shove from Molly that sent her reeling toward the edge of the pit. For an instant, Slocum thought Erin had regained her balance. Then she toppled into the pit. A second later came a loud splash.

"Reckon she ain't dead. Mighty wet, though." Eustace came up behind Slocum and whispered in his ear, "Rot in hell, you mangy dog, you."

Slocum had a split second to prepare for the fall. He silently vowed not to give them the satisfaction of hearing him cry out on the way down. Just as his resolve was wearing thin and he wanted to bellow out in rage, his feet hit the pool at the bottom of the pit. His outcry was cut off by cold black water. He sputtered and shook and struggled to get to the surface with his hands bound behind him.

"John, here. Over here," Erin called to him. "I was lucky. I got my hands free on the way down." She held up her wrists. In the faint light from above Slocum saw her bloodied wrists where she had fought the hemp ropes and won. He struggled to kick hard enough to keep his head above water. Erin saw his plight and grabbed his collar, pulling him over to a rocky ledge.

Slocum got his knees under him and flopped around, out of the water. A shiver seized him. The water had been cold, but the air drying it off his clothing made him even colder.

"Let me get your ropes off. Oh, the knots are all soaked."

"Knife," Slocum said, trying to keep his teeth from chattering. "In my boot top."

The Montroses had missed this weapon when they trussed him up. Erin made quick work of his ropes. He was sorry he hadn't told her to be careful, to cut the ropes so that they might tie long pieces together in an effort to escape the deep pit.

But he was simply happy to get his hands free. Even more so when Erin threw her arms around him and hugged him tight.

"You gave them the map to ransom me," she said. "That's the most wonderful thing anyone's ever done for me."

"The most wonderful thing anyone can do for the two of us is get us out of here," Slocum said. He eyed the steep walls of the pit and wondered what this place was. He didn't see any tunnels leading away. It was as if this was a well with a mighty wide mouth. The sides were slick with slime all twenty feet to the edge.

"We're safe for the moment," Erin said, trying to look on the bright side of their predicament.

"I'm not so sure. It won't be too long before Molly real-
izes there's more to finding the gold than that map."

"She took my coin," Erin said, chagrined at having to
make such a confession. "I don't know if she wanted it because it was gold or if Seamus had mentioned it. But that
witch has it."

"Is she Seamus's sister?" The more he thought on it, the
less he believed she was related to the Preston brothers.
More likely, she had come along and maybe sweet-talked
either Michael or Seamus and had learned of the robbery
that way. Slocum didn't bother to suggest that Seamus
might not have been totally faithful. He knew firsthand how
seductive Molly could be. But his money was on Molly and
Michael making whoopee, since she hadn't known of the
need to use the two half coins to orient the map.

"I find it hard to believe Molly and Seamus were in the
same family. He was so kind, when he thought on it, and
not at all like her. But Michael, well, he and Molly are a bit
alike. Were. Oh, John, I don't know what to do." She broke
down crying, clinging to him. He could do nothing but hold
her for a spell.

As he held her quaking body in his arms, he looked
around and thought hard. Molly might have the entire map
and Erin's half of the coin, but the other half coin still rode
on a rawhide thong around his neck. Eustace had not bothered to search him. After all, the map was all there was to
claim. The Montrose gang had wanted to put an end to him
and Erin so they could get a move on and find the stolen
bullion.

"They might be back. I've still got the other half," he
told her.

"They have us bottled up here. They can kill us and
take it."

"Not if we're gone when they return," Slocum said.
There was a chance Molly and Eustace would never return.
There was no reason for them to think he had the final key

to finding their treasure. Molly wouldn't give up, but she might not think to ask a man she had seen tossed into a watery grave if he held the last piece of the puzzle.

The ropes that had held Erin's wrists together were nowhere to be seen. The ropes she had cut from his wrists lay in small sections around the ledge. Worthless for climbing. But maybe not entirely without some usefulness.

"How wet are these ropes?" Slocum wondered. He released her and twisted the rope hard to get out as much water as he could before peeling apart the strands. Using a lucifer from the watertight tin tucked in his vest pocket, alongside the gold half coin, he set fire to one end. A guttering pale yellow light illuminated their rocky prison.

"There's no way to climb up," Erin said. "The sides are too smooth, even if it weren't for the slime covering everything."

Slocum moved around and held up the sputtering hunk of rope to get as good a look as possible at a spot ten feet above their heads.

"What's that look like? There?" He pointed to the spot he had noticed.

"A mine shaft?"

"This is another glory hole. The roof caved in to an upper level, then kept collapsing. It fell two entire levels."

"But the water. Where'd it come from?"

"If the mine flooded, that might have washed out the supports and caused the collapse all the way to the surface," Slocum said. "That means there might be another tunnel about . . . there."

He estimated distances and pointed to a spot just under the surface of the water.

"If the mine flooded, all the lower drifts will be underwater. And I don't think we can climb to the upper level tunnel. It's too far and the rock is so slick." Erin started to cry.

Slocum might have calmed her, but he was more inclined to find a way out of their predicament. Moaning about their bad luck wasn't going to get them free. Slocum took out his tin of matches and the gold coin and pressed them into Erin's hand.

"Keep these. Till I get back."

"What are you going to do?"

He shucked off his wet boots and stripped off his heavy coat and gunbelt. How light that belt seemed without the three pounds of shooting iron weighing it down. Slocum sucked in a few deep breaths, then jumped into the cold water. He dropped several feet before giving a powerful scissors kick that took him to the far wall. Even in the dark he saw a darker circle in the wall. A tunnel. Stroking forward, he swam deeper into the flooded drift. Lungs approaching the bursting point, he knew he should turn back.

He kept swimming forward.

Then he burst out, gasping for air, into a relatively dry tunnel that sloped upward. Dragging himself out of the water, he lay for a minute regaining his strength and making sure he could breathe without passing out. Sometimes, flooded tunnels were also the home to dangerous pockets of gas. A few tentative sniffs convinced him the air was as good as any he'd ever taken into his lungs.

Making his way up the slope, he turned and let out a yelp of glee. He saw sunlight diffused by heavy storm clouds! Slocum hurried forward and came to a branch in the tunnel. One way led outside. The other curled around where a vagrant vein of ore had been followed religiously. He guessed where it ended.

A dozen paces around the curving tunnel brought him to a sudden drop-off—into the watery well where Erin huddled over the feeble fire of a burning rope, trying vainly to warm herself.

He called down to her. Erin jumped in surprise, then looked upward.

"John! How'd you get up there? Never mind. Get me out of here!"

He decided it was only as a last resort that Erin should try to swim underwater through the tunnel to reach the exit. He had barely made it and wasn't sure he could swim back to get her, then retrace his escape path.

"I'll find a rope or some other way to pull you up. It may take a few minutes, so don't worry."

Before she could urge him to stay for just another minute or two, he ducked back and went exploring in the tunnels. The mine had been abandoned, leaving behind rusty equipment and useless timbers. The rot had set in, making the wood more dangerous than of value in getting Erin out of the pit.

But Slocum did find a winch with a cable still wrapped around its drum. He wrestled it along the tunnel before he realized he could never hold it in place and crank the handle, bringing Erin up. Slocum hunted without finding a decent way of securing the winch. Then he saw a roof timber with supports that appeared sturdy enough for the task. Wedging the winch into the rock behind one roof support, he ran the cable out to the edge of the pit.

"John! How long before you get me out?" Erin sounded a mite frantic.

"I'll fix a loop at the end of the rope. You slide your arms through it so it goes around your body. Then hang on. I'll pull you up. Be sure to bring the matches and the coin."

"Got them here," she said, holding them above her head.

Slocum quickly fixed a sturdy loop that wouldn't slip off the woman's trim body or cut her too badly, then dropped it over the edge. As Erin got the rope secured around her, he returned to the winch. He hoped the timber would hold long enough.

"Ready?" he called. Slocum got her eager reply and began turning the crank handle. Inch by inch the rope was wrapped back around the drum. But after only a few turns he saw how the wooden timber was beginning to yield. The roof was starting to cascade dust down on his head, and the timber support was breaking from the strain.

Slocum cranked faster and the wood began splintering. The winch started to slip past the wood support, but he refused to give up. Slocum braced his body, shoved his feet against the edge of the winch and kept turning as fast as possible. He looked up and knew it was a race against time. The roof might cave in and crush him.

It might do him in, but he wasn't going to strand Erin in that watery grave. Better to die with a ton of rock smashing down on them than to starve to death.

"I'm almost at the edge, John. A little more. Pull me up just a little more!"

The rope snapped, relieving the pressure against the mine support. But Erin was tied onto the other end of the now-slack line.

"Erin!" Slocum called. "Erin!"

He got no answer.

17

Slocum stared at the line on the dusty tunnel floor, then dived and grabbed for it. There was no pressure against the rope.

"Erin!" he called. "Erin!"

He began reeling in the line, until it pulled taut. He frowned and realized that if the line were still around the woman's body, she couldn't be more than a few feet below the lip of the tunnel. Slocum scuttled along the floor, maintaining tension on the rope until he reached the edge of the tunnel.

Erin clung for dear life to a tiny outcropping not a foot below him. She pressed her face hard against the cold, slimy wall and fought in silence to keep from tumbling back down into the well below.

"I'll pull you up," Slocum said, bracing his feet as much as possible. There was scant traction for him, but he applied all the tension on the rope that he could. A sudden jerk brought Erin popping up and over the edge. Slocum crashed onto his back and she fell heavily atop him. He looked up into her face. She still refused to look, and her eyes were screwed tightly shut.

"You can look now," he said. "You're safe."

Erin slowly opened her blue eyes and looked down at him. A smile danced on her lips and she said, "Not that safe, I hope."

"We've got to get out of here." Slocum helped her to her feet and dusted himself off. She stood silently, hand outstretched. In her palm were both the tin of matches and the half of the double eagle that unlocked the location of the stolen bullion.

"Are you sure?" he asked. She nodded, as if she didn't trust herself to speak. Slocum took the lucifers and tucked them into his still-wet pocket. Then he hung the gold coin around his neck again, hiding it under his shirt. No sooner had the coin vanished than Erin threw her arms around his neck and kissed him.

"We can go now," she said. "Lead the way."

Slocum got his bearings, followed the drift for some distance and then found a ladder going to the surface. The mine mouth opened onto a slope a quarter mile from the pit where they had been tossed. The dawn was even more diffused by the clouds roiling over the Sierras, but Slocum had no trouble figuring out where they had to go. He pointed north.

"The town's about ten miles in that direction." He frowned a moment and added, "Be sure to skirt around the Montrose gang's camp on your way there. Tell the sheriff what's happened and have him send out a posse after Eustace and Molly and the rest."

"What're you going to do, John? You aren't thinking of going after them on foot?" Erin sounded shocked at the very idea he would want revenge. Slocum wanted more than that. Molly had the completed map and Erin's part of the coin. If he hotfooted it, he might overtake the gang and get all the details of where the bullion had been hidden before Sheriff George caught up. Slocum was counting on the lawman being out of town and taking a day or two before he rustled up a posse and came charging out of Virginia City.

"I won't leave you," Erin said flatly.

"Don't you want Eustace and the others arrested for kidnapping you?" Slocum hesitated, then added what Erin had to be thinking already. "They must have murdered Seamus, too."

"That bitch might have done it herself. There's no telling what she's capable of."

There was no reason to think Molly wasn't capable of any depth of treachery with a million dollars in gold at stake. Eustace Montrose had better start watching his back once they got close to the gold, because Molly was the sort of gal who would take a fancy to owning it all.

"How do you intend to track them on foot, without any sort of weapon?" Erin demanded.

Slocum drew his trusty knife and balanced it on his fingertips. In spite of the use it had seen, it still balanced perfectly. He didn't need his Colt Navy, as much as he missed it weighing down his left hip, because he was determined not to let Montrose and Molly get away with all they had done. Gold or no gold, they would pay.

"I'll make out," Slocum told her.

"Then you shall do it with me alongside. I owe you that much support. You saved my life, John."

"Get the sheriff. That's what I need."

Erin looked at him. Her blue eyes took on an inner glow in the dim light of the new day.

"You're going to get the gold, aren't you?"

"First things first," he said.

"I'd be forced to think you had only my best interests at heart if I returned to Virginia City and informed the sheriff of your wild-ass chasing after the gang."

Slocum was amused at the way she spoke now. Then he saw how serious she was.

"If you come along, you've got to keep up. I'm going to be moving mighty fast."

"Go on," she said. Erin stood with her chin raised and a defiant look on her lovely face. "Let's see if I can keep up."

Slocum knew she wouldn't be able to maintain his pace as he set off at a dogtrot. He could keep this speed all day long. He lacked the endurance of an Apache or an Ute when it came to such running, especially in the high mountains, but the ground-devouring stride would quickly close the distance between him and the outlaws. The Montrose gang had to stop now and again to be sure they were following the map. When they learned they had no way of finding the gold because the remaining piece of the compass rose dangled around Slocum's neck, they would certainly stop and argue the matter among themselves.

By then, Slocum hoped to be close enough to pick them off one by one.

He fell into an easy lope that soon had Erin panting harshly behind him. Slocum never slackened the pace. He was bound and determined to finish this immediately, if he could. The sun might pop out from behind the heavy clouds and spotlight him, if the Montroses bothered to look at their backtrail. Slocum knew he had only one chance at recovering the map and the gold coin, because the family would unite against him in a flash if they spotted him.

Slocum kept running until he came to a meadow. A wolf growled toward the center of the quarter-mile expanse. Then coyotes howled a warning. Erin staggered up, flushed and almost at the end of her endurance.

"T-taking a break?" she gasped out. "Wondered how much longer you could run."

Slocum was sweaty but not winded. He held her back and pointed to the dark shapes moving restlessly through the meadow.

"That's not good. They're eating something." He mentally added, *or someone.*

"John, over there. Horses. Three or four of them. Did a pack of wolves bring down a horse?"

"You're close to the truth," he said. "I think Montrose or Molly—or both of them—took care of four of his clan. Don't know what happened to the others, but I doubt they're riding with Eustace or Molly any longer."

"What'll we do?"

"We don't disturb dinner, that's for certain sure." Slocum guided her at a deliberate walk in the direction of the frightened horses. It took the better part of twenty minutes before he had captured all four of the animals.

"We can ride in style. If one gets tired, we switch to our spare," he said. Even better than riding, he had one of his six-shooters in his holster again. He had found it in the saddlebags of a big roan, where one of the gang must have stashed it.

"Are you sure we're heading in the right direction, John?" she asked. "Maybe we ought to get the sheriff."

"I can track them just fine," he told her. He knew Erin's problem. She was thinking of the four dead men back in the meadow and what that meant about the man and woman they were going to tangle with. "There're supplies in the saddlebags. Why not camp? I'll finish this off and come back for you."

"Will you?"

"Yes," he said.

"Even if you find the gold?" Before he could answer, Erin rushed on. "Never mind. I'll ride along and keep my yap shut. You won't even know I'm here. I promise."

Slocum shrugged. It would get bloody before the smoke cleared. Watching after Erin was a chore, but he could do it, if he had to. He had promised Michael Preston to deliver the map and had tried. He had eventually found himself thinking more of Erin and keeping her from harm than he ought to. She was a mighty fine-looking woman, had guts and determination, and wouldn't turn tail and run when the shooting started. But he didn't want to be forced to decide between her and a million dollars in gold bars.

He rode slowly to be certain he didn't miss anything left by the riders ahead. Occasionally he dismounted to be sure the riders had not veered away and taken a side canyon. Mostly, they stuck to the main road leading southward. An hour later, he found spoor showing they had turned west and headed into the mountains.

"We're closing in on them," Slocum said, eyeing a pile of fresh horse dung. Montrose and Molly had passed by within the hour.

"Who do you mean?"

"Molly and Eustace," he said. Then he realized he was making an assumption that didn't match what facts he had. All he knew was that four people had died in the meadow. Eustace and Molly might have been half that dinner for scavengers, done in by Eustace's brothers or even his sons. There was no honor among thieves, much less between members of the Montrose family. Then he considered how mad-dog vicious Eustace was and how conniving Molly could be.

"Molly and Eustace," Slocum said with more determination. "They're the two we're following."

"But—"

Slocum held up a hand to silence her. Echoes from deeper in the canyon came out. He listened hard and knew he heard voices, even if he could not make out the words.

"They're arguing," Erin said. "The words are all jumbled up, but they're mad and shouting at each other." She looked at him with new respect. "One voice is shriller than the other."

"Molly's," he said. A deeper voice sent shock waves down the canyon. "And Eustace."

Slocum slid his six-gun from its holster and checked the loads in the cylinder. He was loaded for bear—or Eustace Montrose.

They rode more slowly now, straining to make out the words. The argument rose in pitch, then died down below the whistle of wind blowing through the canyon. By the time the sun was above the mountains behind them, they might have been riding into a deserted canyon.

"Do you think they stopped to eat?" Erin asked. "I'm getting mighty hungry."

"Get some jerky from the saddlebags and gnaw on that. We keep riding." Slocum wanted this over. They had swapped horses several times during their ride from the meadow and had narrowed the gap between them and their quarry to what Slocum estimated to be a mile or two. He doubted Montrose would spend any time worrying about anyone on his backtrail because the glint of gold would lure him on.

Less than a half hour later, Slocum and Erin entered a broad valley where canyons crossed.

"Which way?" Erin looked around and looked confused. "There's a road coming down from the other canyon big enough to take ten wagons with bullion."

Before Slocum could decide which direction Eustace and Molly had gone, he heard a gunshot from the left-hand branch. He looked at Erin, then drew his Colt Navy and put his spurs to his horse's flanks. Erin hung back but not by much. Less than a mile deeper into the canyon Slocum saw a frightened horse, eyes wide and white with fear, galloping past off to his right.

Slocum cocked his six-gun and advanced at a walk.

He drew rein and looked down a slope to the rocky shore of a stream running through the canyon.

"What happened, John?" asked Erin. Then she saw the body and gasped. "Molly!"

"Reckon Eustace figured out that she wasn't going to find the gold with the map and only half the coin."

"They argued earlier. That's what we heard. They argued and he shot her dead!"

"Looks like it," Slocum allowed. He had started to ride deeper into the canyon, when Erin called to him.

"Aren't you going to do anything for her?"

"She's dead," he said. "I doubt Montrose would leave the map and coin half on her. He might not figure out where the gold is actually stashed, but he's not going to leave what clues he has on the likes of her."

"We should bury her. It's the only d-decent thing to do. Otherwise, s-she'll be ea-eaten by coyotes like the others back in the meadow."

"She would have left you to drown or starve to death in that glory hole," Slocum said.

"She would have," Erin said, her courage coming back, "but we're better than that. We should do the right thing."

Slocum thought the right thing was putting a couple rounds into Montrose's putrid heart, but he reluctantly agreed. It took better than a half hour to dig a shallow grave for Molly Preston and cover her with rocks too large for the coyotes to move easily. It was more than she deserved.

"Thank you, John," Erin said. "You know it was what had to be done."

Slocum said nothing. His mind already ranged far and wide, trying to figure how to take down Eustace Montrose. The additional time Montrose had gained since killing Molly gave him several miles' head start. Or did it?

The hair on the back of Slocum's neck rose. Eustace Montrose was close. He felt it.

Slocum motioned Erin to stay back, then put his finger to his lips, cautioning her to silence. He rode a hundred yards deeper into the canyon, hoofbeats muffled by the burbling stream running off to his right. Slocum slowed and finally drew to a halt. He dismounted and walked around a bend in the road, expecting Montrose to be waiting for him with a rifle trained on his head.

Slocum saw the giant of a man hunched over in the middle of the road. Eustace cursed a blue streak as he worked, turning the coin this way and that over the map, then finally throwing down the half coin in a fit of rage.

Slocum reached under his shirt and pulled out the other half of the gold double eagle. He let it swing in the bright sunlight poking through the clouds. A ray flashed across the map and caught Montrose's attention.

Eustace Montrose whipped around, his hand going for the six-shooter hanging at his side.

"You need the other half of the coin, Montrose," Slocum said. "You need this." Slocum held the coin at arm's length in his left hand.

Montrose lifted his six-shooter, but Slocum shot first. His .36-caliber round hit the giant of a man in the middle of his chest. Montrose staggered back a step, looked at the tiny red spot blossoming into a deadly flower on his chest and continued to bring up his six-gun.

Slocum fired again. This time his round hit Montrose in the middle of the forehead, just above the nose he had mashed. The man swung around, facing away from Slocum, took a step and then crashed to the ground, face-down in the dirt.

"You stupid son of a bitch," Slocum said, looking down at the body. "You looked at the gold coin, not the hand holding the gun on you."

He knelt and saw the map held down with rocks at the corners. He retrieved the half of the coin Erin had carried and fitted it together with his.

"You're going after the gold now, aren't you?" Erin looked down at him with a disgusted look on her pretty face.

"Can't hurt to see what that much bullion looks like," Slocum said. "I have to hand it to Molly. She almost had it right." Slocum took the coin, studied it and the surrounding mountains, then aligned it to the west instead of the more usual north—the broad three-line scratch he had thought was a lightning bolt was yet another trick. The scratch on the other half of the coin matched up with an apparently extraneous line on the map to point the way to the gold cache.

"There, across the stream," Slocum said. He bundled up the map and coins and tucked them into his pocket. He mounted and rode in silence to the hillside on the far canyon wall. Slocum was aware how Erin fumed at this excursion, especially since she knew what he would do once he located the stolen bullion.

The ruts left by ten heavily laden wagons showed in the grass once they reached the softer dirt. Slocum's heart beat faster as he saw a small opening in the side of the canyon wall overgrown with blackberry bushes. The wagon tracks leading in had been brushed out with weeds used like crude brooms, but he knew that trick. His heart raced as he realized he had found the gold.

"In there," Slocum said. He gingerly pulled back the thorny bushes and slipped past them. The crevice was hardly wide enough to accommodate a wagon, but it took Slocum only a few minutes of walking to come upon the last one in the wagon train. He jumped up into the wagon bed and looked into the shadows farther ahead. Nine more wagons. He had found the mother lode.

Ripping back canvas on the end wagon, he saw bar after bar of gold. Each weighed forty or fifty pounds, but he also discovered dozens of leather bags of gold dust. A single bag weighed a couple pounds. He could take ten of them and have damned near two thousand dollars' worth of gold in his saddlebags and not even touch the huge stash hidden here.

"It's wrong, John. You can't take this gold. It's stolen property."

"How those San Francisco bankers got it in the first place is certainly a matter to argue, but stealing gold that's been stolen twice seems just fine to me."

"John," she said in a disapproving, schoolmarm tone.

"Here," Slocum said, handing her the map and complete coin. "You take that on back to Virginia City and give it to Sheriff George, if you like. If you think that's the right thing to do, then do it. Don't begrudge me this much."

Slocum left Erin standing in the narrow crevice, staring at the map and coin in her hand. He loaded the gold dust into his saddlebags, then weighed down his spare horse with four bullion bars. Sweating from the work of loading so much gold, he wiped his forehead and looked around to get his bearings. If he kept riding along this canyon, he might come out onto the Nevada desert. With a bit of hard riding, he might beat the coming storms and reach Denver in time to find a nice place to spend the winter.

He reached the road, looked down at Eustace Montrose's body and figured that the coyotes might puke if they ate him. Slocum had nothing against coyotes and buzzards. He dismounted and buried the man, wishing him a speedy journey to hell.

Slocum mounted and was hardly on the road leading to Denver when he heard hoofs pounding behind him. He looked over his shoulder. A flushed Erin Finnigan pulled up beside him.

"I'm glad I caught you, John."

"Why's that?"

"I thought real hard for a spell back there and came to a decision." She patted her bulging saddlebags, then fumbled in a pocket and handed him half the map and half the gold coin. "In case we want to find the gold again. I don't know how long a few thousand dollars will last me—or you."

Slocum laughed, leaned over and kissed her full on the lips. They'd have a hell of a fine time spending the gold. And if they spent it all, they could return to get more.

Together.

Watch for

SLOCUM'S SWEET REVENGE

316th novel in the exciting SLOCUM series
from Jove

Coming in June!

Explore the exciting Old West with one of the men who made it wild!

J. R. ROBERTS

THE GUNSMITH